CONCLAVE

CONCLAVE

NEW YORK TIMES BESTSELLING AUTHOR
PENELOPE DOUGLAS

ALSO BY PENELOPE DOUGLAS

THE FALL AWAY SERIES
Bully

Until You

Rival

Falling Away

Aflame

Next to Never

(includes novellas Aflame and Next to Never)

STAND-ALONES
Misconduct

Birthday Girl

Punk 57

Credence

Tryst Six Venom

THE DEVIL'S NIGHT SERIES
Corrupt

Hideaway

Kill Switch

Conclave

(novella)

Nightfall

Fire Night

(novella)

AUTHOR'S NOTE

Conclave is a 27,000 word novella that takes place between *Kill Switch* and *Nightfall*. It is a spoiler for every book in the Devil's Night series, and it is available for FREE on my website at https://pendouglas.com/ in the BONUS section. You do not have to pay for it. However, if you're a Devil's Night lover, I've made this available in ebook and paperback for those of you who wanted it for your collections. Enjoy!

PART 1

Damon

I walk in, dropping my keys on the entryway table as I pass on my way to the kitchen. I dart my eyes up.

There are no lights on upstairs.

If she left me, I'm going to burn the whole fucking world down until I find her, and if she took my kid, I'm really going to take my time with her. This is bullshit. *When I call, you answer. When my men pass you the phone, you take the goddamn call!* I have no idea what the hell I did now, but I'm going to have to break something to keep myself from wringing her precious, little neck.

Cutting my trip short to race home, because she decides to ignore my calls and do little pirouettes all over my peace of mind? What the fuck? I knew I should've been single. I knew that I knew that, because this is what women do, isn't it? They take you and ball you up into a nice, little, fucking knot until you can't breathe, and...

I clench my fists, shaking my head. *Bullshit.* This is such bullshit!

I charge down the hall toward the kitchen, ready to hit the attached garage and grab myself some rope to remind her whom she's in love with, but I spot a figure out on the patio and stop.

It's raining outside. Who's there?

I change directions and head for the windows.

Heath Davis, one of the guards Mr. Garin hired for the night shift, leans against the bricks of the house, shielded from the rain under the awning. His hands sit in his pockets and a cigarette hangs out of his mouth. Smoke billows into the air above his head, and I lick my lips, trying to ignore the burning need on my tongue. The problem with quitting smoking is it's really hard if you never fully quit.

His black hair, neatly combed back, shines under the flaming porch light, and his blue eyes are turned toward the yard, watching something.

I follow his gaze.

Winter stands waist deep in the pool, her back to us as droplets pummel the surface of the water and her hair sticks to her back.

I release a breath I didn't realize I was holding. She's here.

She raises her arms, gliding them through the evening rain as she steps to the right, and then swings out her arms and steps to the left.

She's dancing. She practices in the pool a lot for balance.

But then, I watch as she pulls all of her hair to one side, revealing her naked back, and I drop my eyes down her spine to her naked waist and hips.

I dip my chin, my eyes going hot. She's not wearing any clothes.

I move just my eyes, darting them over to Davis. He doesn't blink, his gaze staying on her.

When I said watch her every minute, I didn't mean that.

2

Winter turns around, still fisting her hair with both hands, so her arms are covering her breasts, but I notice the white tulle she wears covering her face, and my heart feels like it's skipping ten beats. It's part of the costume for her upcoming show, and she'll practice with it to get used to it.

But only wearing that and no clothes—and as far as she knows, I'm not here to see it—really pisses me off.

I watch as she drops her arms and sways to the side, shooting out her hands and twirling in the rain. Her wild hair, the see-through fabric on her face, her perfect breasts and skin...

God, she's fucking surreal. With something about her that will always be innocent. Thunder cracks overhead, splitting the sky, and I no longer care if she's angry or why. I want in that pool.

Heading over to the fridge, I pull a sandwich off the tray inside and take a butcher knife out of the block, slicing the square in half before walking outside. I take a bite with the knife still in my other hand.

Davis notices me right away and straightens, stomping out his cigarette. I stare out at Winter, her slender body arching and bending and taunting the fuck out of me like she's so good at doing. My dick swells in my pants, and I cast him a quick glance. I'll bet his is good and hard, too.

Davis clears his throat. "You said to watch her every minute."

I take another bite and scrape the blade across the wrought-iron fence, cleaning the mustard off.

"Excuse me, sir." And I see him dip his head out of the corner of my eye and back away to leave.

But I stop him. "Give me your belt."

He pauses. "Sir?"

I sheath the knife in the flower pot in front of me, stabbing the soil.

He clears his throat again, and I hear a jangling as he quickly removes his leather belt.

He holds it out for me, and I take it. "If you ever insult my wife again," I tell him, "I'll take my son fishing using your eyeballs as bait."

"Yes, sir."

It's not Winter's fault. She's in her home, it's late, and she should be able to expect privacy.

I fling the rest of the sandwich into the bushes and slide the end of the belt through the buckle. "Go home," I tell him.

After a moment, I hear the back door open and close, and I head for the pool deck, belt in hand.

Raining, dark, enclosed by trees…I stalk toward her, quiet and calm. It's like we're kids again. I love being hidden with her outside.

Winter dances slowly, her movements long and languorous with no real choreography as she freestyles to the soft, haunting tune coming from the pool house. Her wet skin glimmers in the faint glow coming from the house, and I don't take my eyes off her as I strip off my clothes.

Leaving them in a pile on the ground, I grip Davis's black, leather belt in my hand and hop in the pool. She stops moving, turning her head at the sound, but she doesn't face me or say anything.

She knows it's me.

Threading the strap through my fist, I walk through the heated water, taking in the glittering droplets on her shoulder blades as the rain hits my own head and arms.

I stop right behind her, the top of her head resting under my chin.

"I have something for you." I lean down, grazing her ear with my lips. "You want it?"

But she turns her head away.

I cock an eyebrow, widening the gap in the belt.

"You must be very angry," I say. "I call, you don't answer. I send flowers—fucking flowers, Winter—and I don't even get a text. I tap into the cameras, and you have them offline…"

She refuses to turn around.

I drop the loop over her head and pull the slack tight, her body slamming back into mine.

She gasps, and I look down, seeing her breasts rise and fall quickly.

I dip down again. "What did I do now, huh?" I growl low in her ear.

But she whips around, the belt slipping through my hand as she sloshes through the pool and away from me.

I grind my teeth together, following her with my eyes. She stands up tall again, defiant with her hands on the surface of the pool in front of her, so she can feel me coming.

The strap of the belt wraps around her neck, the slack falling down her back, and while I can barely make out her eyes, I see her pink lips, panting through the wet fabric.

"Not talking to me?" I start to circle her. "Hmm…I must've done something very bad."

Her hair sticks to one of her breasts, and I can almost feel them between my lips.

And I no longer give a shit what she's mad about, because I want her in our bed.

"Come here," I tell her.

But she moves away instead, sensing my approach.

"Come here, Winter," I say more firmly.

She continues to circle as I circle, the rain dancing across the pool and splashing up onto her stomach. Every inch of her skin is drenched, and my mouth is suddenly so dry.

"Now."

But she tips her chin up a little, keeping her lips good and closed.

I grin, hoping she can hear it in my voice, because I'm losing my fucking patience. "Your sister came when she was called," I taunt.

And that is it. Winter's icy façade suddenly cracks. Her eyes go wide and then quickly morphs into a glare as she shoots out both hands and shoves water at me.

I dive in and grab her as she's distracted, throwing her over my shoulder. "Such a troublesome girl," I scold, slapping her ass. "Why couldn't I like the easy one? But no, I wanted *this* one."

I hold her in my arms, but she arches back up, facing down at me with a scowl as she pushes at my chest.

Darting out my tongue, I run it up her stomach, licking off the water. A whimper escapes her, but she turns her head away, playing defiant.

My dick is ready to go, but it's funny. As mad as she gets me, I secretly love it. I like it when it's not easy. I take some skin between my teeth, looking up to see her eyes close as she digs her nails in my shoulders.

"Yell at me," I whisper. "Scream. Hit me."

I grip her ass in my hands, keeping my eyes on her as I graze the underside of her breast with my mouth.

"You mad at me?" I say against her skin, seeing her nipples, erect and hard for me.

She says nothing.

My lips tickle her breasts as I continue taunting her. "You want to leave and find yourself a decent man?"

She doesn't want someone else. She better not want someone else. She likes me misbehaved. She likes me, period.

She still doesn't answer, but she's no longer pushing me away.

I quirk a smile. "You wanna touch me?"

When she doesn't say anything, I shift her to one arm and grab the belt at her back with my free hand and pull, forcing her neck back as I catch one nipple between my teeth.

She gasps. "Damon."

I nibble hard, biting into her breast and sucking on it as her clit throbs against my stomach.

"You hate me?" I play, walking to the edge of the pool and dropping her to her feet. "You done with me? Is that it?"

I push her into the wall, seeing a smile peek out before she quickly hides it again.

"You hate what I do to you?"

She bites her bottom lip, breathing hard.

I whip her around, wrapping my arm around her waist as I press her into the pool edge and breathe hot into her hair. My dick is so hard, I can already feel it dripping.

"Talk to me," I tell her.

Reaching around, I tip her chin up toward me and cover her mouth through the fabric, an electric current shooting through me at the feel of her tongue brushing my lips, but I can't get at it, because of the tulle. My whole body hurts. I need her.

"Talk to me," I whisper against her mouth. "Please."

She keeps silent.

I nibble her lips, sliding my hand down her ass and teasing that little spot that scares her just a little.

She shudders as I push her forward and force her knee up onto the step. She leans onto the pool deck as I rub her clit with one hand and her ass with the other. My dick naturally finds where to go, pressing into her tight, little entrance.

I see her gulp.

"Talk to me," I warn her. "If you want to stop me..."

Then you're going to have to ask.

Her jaw flexes as she keeps her mouth shut, and I'm not even mad. I don't want to stop. The rain falls around us, and I lean down, sucking the water off her back as the head of my cock presses into her, and I hear her whimper as I push through her tight little opening and stop.

"Damon," she pants, her chin trembling nervously at where I'm going. "Damon..."

But I clamp my hand over her mouth and pull her back to me, her back arching so goddamn beautifully, and I'm not even all the way inside her yet.

"You had you your chance," I whisper in her ear. "My turn."

I slowly slide the rest of the way in, taking it in stride as much for me as for her. She needs to adjust, but she's so damn tight I'll be done before we even start.

I bury myself to the hilt, feeling the cool skin of her ass pressed into my hips, and I pause for a moment to let her get used to it. Her body shakes in my arms, but as soon as her breathing starts to slow, I start moving.

Gliding in and out, shallow at first, I feel her constrict around me, and I'm reeling. I don't care what I did. I'd happily take an eight-hour flight for this. All she has to do was ask.

After a minute, I feel her start to back up into it, meeting me halfway, and I remove my hand from her mouth.

"Don't talk," I tell her. "Just take it."

I grip her hip in one hand and the belt with the other and fuck her tight, little ass, taking out all the frustration she causes me that I love. I kiss and bite her neck and lips, eating her up as I sink my body into hers with her moans filling my ears.

"Decent men don't do this," I tell her. "But that's why I wanted *this* one. She's a devil, just like me."

She digs her nails into the pool deck, her neck pulled back by the belt, and I look down, watching my dick slide in and out of her as her wet hair bounces against her ass.

"Harder," she moans.

I take her hand and put it on her clit, watching her arm move quick as she rubs herself, while I fuck her.

Her moans get louder, I feel her body shake, and I pound harder as I pull the belt as taut as I can.

She screams, and I'm immediately behind her, coming with three more hard thrusts and every muscle burning to exhaustion.

Oh, God. My whole body fires up, my stomach explodes with pleasure, and I release the belt, letting her fall forward before I break her neck. She lays over the edge, whimpering and breathing hard, and I unclench my fingers from her hips, withdrawing my nails from her skin.

She whines a little when I slide out of her, but I don't move otherwise. Leaning down, I rest my forehead into her back.

"I love you," I say.

She doesn't respond, and I'm too weak to keep up the pretense.

"Okay, okay," I admit. "Yeah, I may have threatened your choreographer with..." I search for words that won't piss her off, "removal of certain limbs. I don't like him putting his hands there. I put my hands there."

He doesn't need to hold her that far up her inner thigh, for Christ's sake, I don't care what the lift is called or if he's gay. Just no.

"They all need to fucking know," I explain. "They'll respect you, and they will respect me, so by the time Ivarsen is old enough to notice, they won't need to be reminded again." I stand up and turn her around, guiding her legs around me as we float back into the pool. "The only one who can bring Ivar Torrance's father to his knees is Ivar's mother."

I want them all to respect me. He doesn't touch my wife like that, and if that means they fear me, then okay.

She purses her lips to one side, looking unimpressed but not really angry anymore.

I rub her nose with mine. "Forgive me?"

She lets out a sigh but then slowly nods.

I smile, relieved. "Talk to me, then?"

But then she shakes her head.

I growl and push back, letting her go. "Then, if that's not it, what the hell did I do?" I slap the water. "Goddammit!"

She stands up, replying flatly, "You won the bet."

And then she turns around, finding the edge of the pool and hops out.

The bet...

It only takes a moment for the light to dawn, and I realize what she's talking about. The bet. My chest swells, and a smile spreads across my face as I dive for the edge of the pool, catching up with her.

"And you let me fuck you like that?" I scold, hopping out of the pool and lifting her up again.

Her arms and legs wrap around me, and I gaze up at her beautiful face as she strips off the mask and the belt.

"Yes, because I needed that," she admits, looking embarrassed. "You know I'm all over you in the first trimester, especially."

I laugh and squeeze her harder. I never actually thought I'd succeed. After Ivarsen was born, I wanted to keep going. Kids in our twenties, raise them in our thirties, and ship them off to college in our forties when we're still young enough to have the house to ourselves and still be kinky, you know?

But she read some study that gifted children are usually only children or in families where the kids are five years or more apart. She wanted Ivar to have our complete attention during his formative years or some shit.

So, we made a bet. She would get pregnant if I could get her pregnant. While she was on birth control.

I knew I was Superman.

"You're mad you're pregnant again?" I tease.

"I'm mad I lost the bet," she snaps.

I kiss her. "Do you really think I'd not let you have something you wanted?"

She smiles. "Really?"

"You want a motorcycle; you get a motorcycle."

Her face lights up with her beautiful, excited smile, and it's the best thing I've ever seen. I can't wait to take her out in the middle of the night on the empty roads.

After the baby comes, of course.

"I love you," she finally says back.

"Good."

I let her down, and we both walk to the pool house, grabbing towels laid out under the awning.

"And in all fairness, I wasn't trying to cut your trip short," she explains. "I'm sorry. I was just making you mad enough that you'd hunt me down when you got home."

A mischievous smile spreads over her face.

Honestly, I don't even care anymore. Michael and Kai can handle the meetings, and I love the angst in the games

Winter and I play. When we're in bed—or the pool—it never feels like we left high school. We're perpetually two horny teenagers, and I feel alive in my life every day.

I wrap a towel around my waist. "Has he been good?"

"Yeah." She nods. "The nanny wanted to give him a sliver of chocolate to see his reaction, but I told her we needed to wait for you."

Hell yes. First chocolate? That's big.

Winter was timid about having a nanny at first, guilty that she couldn't do everything herself, but it's been good. It gives us a little more time alone here and there, too.

She covers herself, and I take her hand. "Come on. I wanna see him."

I know he's asleep, but it's been a week.

But she digs in her heels, stopping us. "He's, um…"

I look at her, my nerves instantly firing. "What?"

"He's, um…" She swallows. "Not here."

Excuse me?

"He's not here?" I repeat. "He's twelve months old, Winter. Where is he?"

She shifts on her feet. "Rika wanted him for the night."

"Rika…" I say. "And she took him to Meridian City?"

Winter turns her head away, telling me all I need to know.

I nod and grab her hand, leading her back to the house. "Of course not."

. . .

Minutes later, we're in the car and racing down the road, heading for the Fane house. I can't believe they'd do this while I was away. If I hadn't come back tonight, would I ever have known?

Winter sits up, dressed in jeans and a navy-blue sweater, her wet hair combed and in a tight ponytail as she faces my direction. "Don't be mad at me."

"You know how I feel about this," I tell her, grinding the wheel in my fist. "There's no one else on my side. Not even Nik. You need to stand by me on this."

"I am," she rushes out. "I just...I don't know." A look of guilt crosses her face. "I guess I felt sorry for her. Rika said she'd be there every minute. I wouldn't put him in danger, Damon."

His "grandmother" is danger.

I want to be angry with Winter. She, above anyone else, should stand by me. She knows why I don't want Ivarsen around Christiane, and it's for good fucking reason.

But it's not like I don't go behind her back to educate her choreographer from time to time or see to it that her old pal Ethan suddenly lost his interest in photography.

But this is our son, dammit. They don't get to make decisions about him without me. Rika has no business sticking her nose in this.

"You know she can't prove herself if you don't give her a chance," Winter points out.

"She had a chance."

After a short pause, Winter adds, "Yeah, so did we." Her voice is somber as we both stare out the windshield. "Thank goodness we gave each other another one."

$$\bullet \bullet \bullet$$

I storm through the dark house, holding Winter's hand, and spot Rika standing outside the library, looking through the windows in the closed doors. A couple of other people stand next to her, and I charge over, the sight of Christiane holding a sleeping Ivar in her arms as she sits in a chair coming into view beyond the glass. A man is in the room with her, reading quietly on the sofa as she rocks my kid.

I reach out and grab the handle, but Rika twists around and steps in front of me, covering my hand with hers.

"Move," I order her.

"She's not hurting him."

"That's right. She won't."

"Damon, calm down," the guy next to her says.

I look over, seeing Will's cousin, Misha.

I glare at him. "Eat my dick."

Winter groans at my side, and some chick with Misha comments, "Oh, so this is Damon."

But I turn my anger back on Rika.

She stares up at me, holding my stare. "Misha?" she says. "Will you give us a second?"

Yes, please. Piss off.

Winter slides out of my hand. "Misha, can you show me the sun room?" she asks him and then to us, "I'll let you two have at it. Sorry, Rika."

"Sorry for putting you in the middle, Winter," Rika tells her.

They leave, and I try to push past her, my eyes darting from her to Ivar.

"That kid doesn't absolve you." Rika inches in front of me again, trying to catch my eyes. "He doesn't make your past go way or make you better than her."

I get in her face, gritting out. "Move."

But she doesn't. "You tied me to a bed," she says. "Kissed me. Bit me. Even as I cried."

The memory of all the times I tried to hurt her—did hurt her—rushes at me, but I push them away.

"Wanted to share me with your friends," she goes on. "Wanted me to yourself for a little while, too, remember that?"

My stomach knots. What the hell?

"Your little sister..." she taunts.

I grab her arm and pull her away from the doors, shoving her into the wall. "You shut up about that shit," I whisper, seething down at her. "I never want to hear about it again."

"You threw me on the ground and tried to take off my clothes..."

I rear back, running my hand through my hair. What the fuck? I thought we were okay. Why is she doing this?

"I didn't want you," she continues to fucking talk, "but you forced your mouth on me anyway."

Taking her by the wrist, I pull her into the kitchen, her bare feet stumbling across the hardwood floors. I force her into the wall and glare down at her.

"I would never have done anything," I growl, no longer keeping my shit to a whisper. "I would never have hurt you!"

"I know."

She answers so quickly and so easily that I hesitate, because I expected her to argue.

She knows. She knew.

Well, at least there's that. But still... She can't compare Christiane to me. We're not the same. Yes, I made enough mistakes to last a lifetime, but I'm not a bad parent, and that's just about the worst thing you can be.

And she was bad for twenty-three consecutive years. Not only did she completely abandon her child, but she put me in the hands of people who were evil.

I made my mistakes when I was young. When I was angry. When I was…alone.

I'm not those things anymore.

What does Christiane have to say for herself, huh?

"And I know you never will hurt me," Rika tells me, her eyes soft and glistening. "I trust you. So, trust me."

I narrow my eyes, part of me wanting to give her what she wants. It's only fair, and I want to trust her.

But she's too good at getting what she wants out of me. Of sacrificing her queen to get my king.

We stare at each other, her words hanging in the air, but then I hear a ringing, and she raises her fingers to her ear, tapping on her earpiece.

"Erika Fane," she answers the phone, holding my eyes. "Charles, so nice to hear from you."

A glint hits her eyes, and I stand up straight, but she stays glued to the wall, watching me as she talks.

"Yes, my assistant sent the itinerary. I can't wait." She smiles.

I slowly release the knots in my stomach, calming my breathing as I wait for her.

Charles…itinerary… She's been busy, trying to finish her degree and mayor the town. It's impressive, though. Putting her into position was one of the better ideas I've ever had.

"Oh, rest assured our future alumni are in good hands," she tells whoever she's talking to. "I'll be there early." She laughs as I hear a male voice on the other end. "Oh, yeah, you know me. Overprepared every time."

I watch her, graceful and well-spoken. A true player.

"No, Michael is in London," she tells him. "But keep his seat open." She eyes me. "I might still be escorted."

I almost snort. As in moi?

Bitch just took my king. She knows I want this. Escorting her to a function in Thunder Bay. Making a public appearance at a respectable event. Having my wife, my kids, and my sisters around me as I slowly build my family and our world, so that when my kid—my children—are old enough to remember, they won't know it was any other way.

She does trust me. God, I don't know why, but...she did let me go when she could've turned me in. And then she rescued me and bled for me and fought with me...

"I know what you do to parents who hurt you," she finally says, returning to our discussion. "Do you really think I'd put her in your path if I weren't sure?"

My mouth curls a little, amused. "You scared of me?"

"Oh, lots." She nods exaggeratedly.

I laugh and turn around, relaxing a little as I walk to the sink and fill up a glass of water.

I gulp down all of it as she pulls some things out from the refrigerator.

She pulls her hair up into a bun and takes out a slice of bread, scooping some tuna onto the slice.

A hunger pang hits at the smell, and I realize all I had to eat today was that half sandwich a half hour ago. Coming to stand at her side, I take a slice out, too, and scoop some tuna salad onto the bread.

"Charles," I repeat the name of whom she was just talking to. "Kincaid?"

As in our old dean, who's still dean of Thunder Bay Prep and helped Winter's father take me down the morning I was arrested?

Rika smiles to herself, and I look down to see her take her single slice filled with tuna and fold it in half, peeling off the top crust. I falter, glancing down at my sandwich, which is already folded the same way. Huh.

"I'm giving the orientation speech tomorrow for the incoming seniors," she explains, taking a bite.

"And Michael and Kai are in London," I add, "trying to wrangle that architect."

I was there, too, until Winter decided to be funny.

So Rika had no one to escort her, except me.

She trails around the island, sitting down on a stool.

She props her elbows up on the counter. "I mean, you don't have to escort me," she explains. "I'm perfectly capable of taking care of myself. And the Andersons will be there, not to mention Kincaid still hates you, so..."

Is she trying to get me excited?

"You just might steal the show." She feigns a sigh, sounding forlorn. "And I know how you like to keep a low profile."

I chuckle, peeling off my crust. She's as good as Winter at playing me, but I can't say I don't enjoy it.

But...I also know she wants a show of trust, too.

I don't want Ivarsen around Rika's mother. But I'm not entirely sure it's because I don't trust her.

Maybe I want to punish her. Maybe I'm jealous that he gets to have what I didn't.

I stare down at the sandwich I can no longer eat, my stomach churning and the hint of bile in my throat.

If I want Rika, and I want my kids to have her, there's no getting around Christiane. I don't want to have to explain to them why they can't see her or why they can't come here.

Fucking fine.

"He can stay the night," I tell her, "and we'll see how it goes."

She's silent, but I can see her looking at me out of the corner of my eye. "Anything beyond that goes through me." I look over at her. "You understand?"

She nods.

And if Christiane disappoints me, she will meet her maker before she ever meets another kid of mine.

I toss the sandwich down on the counter, filling up another glass of water. I have to get this taste out of my mouth.

"Winter's pregnant again, isn't she?" Rika asks, taking another bite.

"How did you know?"

She shrugs. "She's been tired. Nauseous."

Well, that explains why she took the cameras offline then. She didn't want me to see.

Rika leans on the counter, her eyes downcast as she plays with the rest of her sandwich. Her throat moves up and down as she swallows and then her jaw flexes like she's deep in thought.

I take a drink and then dump out the rest of the water. "What?"

She darts her eyes up. "Nothing."

But she's not convincing. She's thinking something.

"What?" I grit out again.

But she fires back. "Nothing."

Her gaze falls to her sandwich again, and I decide to leave it. She knows how to solve her problems.

Which reminds me...

"While we're on the subject, I want you married before you have his child."

She laughs at me. "You want?"

I nod. "Kai married Banks in a day. What's taking so long?"

It was a little different when she was just my friend's girlfriend, but things have changed.

"You're not married to Winter yet, either."

"Winter and I are waiting for Will to come home," I point out.

"Yeah, me, too," she quickly replies, as if latching onto the first viable excuse I was stupid enough to give her.

But that's not it. I know it's not it. They've been engaged for a while, and Will only left town about a year ago. At first, I thought it was Michael. His schedule, his obligations, etc.

I'm not sure it's his fault anymore, though. What's going on with her?

I watch her play with her bread, remembering the first time we were alone in a kitchen together. I had to be fifteen. She saw me, stopped breathing, and left as quickly as possible.

Now she rarely makes a move without my knowledge or input.

"You know what a papal conclave is?" I ask.

She shakes her head a little. "Um, kind of, I guess."

I slide my hands into my pockets and lean against the fridge. "When it's time to elect a new pope, every cardinal in the college of cardinals under the age of eighty is locked in a room until they can come to an agreement on who the new pope will be," I explain. "They started doing this, because eight-hundred years ago, it took three years to choose a new pope due to political infighting. People don't solve problems if they're not forced to face them, you know? Now, the cardinals are led into the Sistine Chapel, there's a shout of 'extra omnes' meaning 'everyone out', and the doors are chained shut, locking them in until they solve the problem."

We might not make the best decisions under pressure, but you can't make a decision at all when you're not talking about it.

She sits there, the wheels in her head turning. "Conclave," she murmurs to herself.

"It's a good idea when you've got things to settle, you know?"

We have weddings to plan. Projects that can't stall, because her fiancé is always out of town. Winter wants to start some humanitarian organization, and I know Kai's family has connections abroad who can help.

Not to mention Banks. We need everything nicely set up for my plans for her, and it's past time to get started. I'll need help getting her on board.

And keeping Kai out of my way about it.

And, of course, there's Will.

"Pithom," she says.

I meet her eyes, a smile spreading across my lips. Michael's family's yacht. Not a bad location. No need for locked doors, because there's no escape at sea.

I nod.

Someone enters the room, and I look up to see Misha walk in, Winter holding onto the other girl's arm.

"I need to talk to you," he says to Rika.

She slides off the stool. "Right," she says, like they had a conversation I interrupted when I showed up. "I'm sorry."

I take Winter's hand and guide her over to me, locking eyes for a moment with the chick who brought her in.

"Who is she?" I ask.

But Misha takes the woman's arm and slides her behind him, out of my view.

I snort. "I just wanted to say hi," I tease. "I mean, we'll all run into each other a lot. She may as well get to know me."

If his dad is dating Rika's mother, and they possibly get married, we'll all have to get really friendly.

Winter chimes in. "His bite is worse than his bark, but he only bites me," she assures the new kids. "Don't worry." And then she arches up on her toes to kiss my jaw. "Get along, please."

Misha's snotty little glare rests on me, because he wouldn't know a good time if it sat on his face. The girl is cute, though.

He finally turns his eyes to Rika. "When was the last time you heard from Will?"

My stomach coils at the mention. Will is rarely in touch these days, but he is adamant that he needs to do what he needs to do. I left him once, after all. If he could wait me out, I can do the same for him.

"He texts," Rika answers.

"He texts you?"

"Well, his parents," Rika replies. "They say he's on a retreat. Doing humanitarian stuff in Asia."

Misha shakes his head. "They're lying."

"How do you know?" I chime in.

"Because I know them," he shoots back. "His mother nods a lot when she's saying things that aren't true."

Rika looks at me. "Rehab?"

Possibly. They could be getting him sober and keeping it quiet.

But it's Misha who responds. "They would tell us, because they know Will would anyway once he got out."

"They might not want us looking for him, though," Rika suggests.

"Well, I think we should," Misha tells her.

I thin my eyes, liquid heat running down my arms, because now he has me afraid.

"Why are you worried?" I ask him.

"Because my grandfather is coming up on re-election, and Will is a mess."

The weight of what he's suggesting slowly starts to sink in. My father threatened me with it countless times, but I've never heard of anyone actually being sent there. He'd be in more danger there than not.

But...he'd be out of the way. He'd be unheard and unseen. No longer a liability.

"Ivar was born a year ago." I look down at Rika as I hold Winter's hand, realization hitting me. "He wouldn't have abandoned me this long. Not willingly."

She shakes her head. "They wouldn't..."

"I really hope not," I say. "Even if we can find it, we'll never get in."

Misha moves up, standing directly at Rika's side. "Don't you worry about it," he tells me. "We'll take care of it."

What? We'll take care of...

I grab Rika's arm and pull her over to my side as I glare at him. "That's right. *We* will."

You little shit. You know what your parents almost married makes you and her? Absolutely nothing. No one shuts me out.

"This is family business," he maintains.

"And I'm the oldest," I fire back, inching forward. "Get in line."

He may very well be her step-brother at some point, but I'm blood.

"Guys..." Rika shoots out her hands to push us both back.

"You fucked him up enough," Misha warns, meeting me eye to eye, "and I'm not twelve anymore."

"Yeah, I know." I smile, giving him a pat on the cheek. He jerks away. "You grew into a pretty young thing, didn't ya, Princess?" I flick the earring in his lip. "You wear more jewelry than a chick, but let's get one thing clear. The only thing those pathetic tattoos serve to do is hide that baby soft skin underneath."

He smirks. "Turning you on, am I?"

His girl snorts behind him, and I scowl.

Misha pushes forward, ignoring Rika's protests. "You're bad for him."

"I didn't let him O.D. to his death on my watch," I growl, throwing the death of his sister in his face.

Misha shoves me in the chest, forcing me back, and the next thing I know, we're both on the ground, scrambling to get on top of each other and punch the living daylights out of one another.

Okay, that was low. Annie was sweet and all. Honestly. But he has some nerve suggesting he'll take care of Will better after what happened to his kid sister. What a little shit.

And to even suggest that he, Rika, and Will are "family business" that doesn't involve me makes me want to grind my boot into his pretty, little, fucking face.

"That's enough!" Rika yells.

I feel people around us as the girls probably scramble to pull us away from each other, but he's had this fucking coming. Wallowing around town in his own personal black parade, all woe is me, because he has a good dad and money and a safe home life, but turning up his nose at it in his hippie search for truth.

"Stop it!"

Someone pulls at my shoulders as I almost get him under me, so I can straddle the little fucker and then maybe he can write a poem about it.

But then ice-cold water hits us both, and I gasp, pausing long enough for Rika to kick me off from him. I fall to the side, both of us breathing hard.

Shit. My hair hangs in my eyes, and I wipe the water out of my eyes.

"Misha," she grits out, staring down at him. "We're having a conclave in one month. You just got yourself invited."

And she stalks off, setting the glass pitcher down on the island.

Misha sits up, flipping me the finger. "Prick."

I push myself to my feet. "Babysoft."

Sea is a great place to bury bodies, you know? Deep breath, asshole.

. . .

Rika

I blow out the smoke, most of it filtering out the window. Normally, I'd go outside, but it's still raining, and I'm too frazzled to care about one cigarette in the house.

Misha. Damon. Will.

Student. Mayor. Aunt.

Sister.

I drop my eyes, taking another drag.

Michael.

I want to do all of it. I hope I can do everything else I want to do, too.

A lump lodges in my throat at the thought of Damon's conclave. There are things I need to say before I leave that boat, but I'm scared.

"I kind of regretted you never grew up with siblings," my mother says, approaching my back, "and now that you have one, he's an immediate bad influence."

She wraps an arm around my waist and smiles at me, cocking an eyebrow at the cigarette in my hand. I laugh, grinding it out in the dish I brought over. Damon and I have stashes in several locations, but none here. I guess if Ivar spends more time here, Damon will, too. May as well arrange one more stash, then.

I look down at the old black and white photos in silver frames adorning the little table in front of me.

My great-grandfather, circa 1900, sits on a horse at the family ranch in South Africa.

I run my finger over his ten-year-old face, the black hair and eyes like coal in the photo. "Ivarsen has the hair," I remark. "Not the eyes, though."

Ivarsen's eyes are blue, like his mother's.

"No," my mother replies. "It skips several generations. None of yours or Damon's children will have both."

My children. A sinking feeling aches in my stomach.

I take a breath and pull away from my mother, giving her a quick kiss on the cheek.

"I'll take the baby monitor in my room," I tell her. "I want to get up with him if he wakes."

And I start to walk away.

"When are you going to tell him?" she calls out.

I stop. But I don't turn around, my heart beating faster. "Tell him what?"

"That your father's will accounted for you *and* any other children I'd have," she says. "When are you going to tell Damon?"

My shoulders relax. Oh, that.

I was pretty pissed when she first told me. I didn't trust him. I wasn't going to allow him to run my father's work into the ground in some temper tantrum. I needed to make sure I could trust him.

In the meantime, I set aside his half in a trust for Ivar, but...

I guess my mother's right. He'll make something out of it. If he wants it.

But I have a feeling he doesn't. I'm kind of proud of him. He's the only one out of the four who can say they're completely self-made. Damon is doing well. I kind of envy the freedom he has. He's creating his own legacy.

But still...he should know. I was wrong to keep it from him.

"I'll deal with it," I tell her and continue walking.

What's one more order of business to add to the conclave anyway? Nine friends locked on a boat with alcohol, spear guns, and the black ocean at night? This was a fantastic idea.

PART 2

Rika

ONE MONTH LATER...

I head down the long, dark corridor, the engines humming under my feet as I pass by the cabins on the yacht. It feels like I'm alone on board, but I know I'm not. This boat will always give me the creeps, I think.

I reach the end of the hall and pull out my AirPods, leaning my ear into the final door and listening.

But I don't hear anything. I grip the handle and slowly twist it, cracking the door open.

A form lays in the bed, under the covers, and I slip inside, leaving the lights off as I set my phone and earbuds down.

I look over at her.

The fading light of the day seeps through the blinds, casting a striped shadow over Alex's body, and I walk toward her and softly climb on the bed, straddling her on my hands and knees.

I look down at her. She's the only one who can make me smile lately. I study her face, taking in her flawless skin and long lashes. Her pert nose and rosy apple cheeks. Her calm breathing and how her eyes don't move behind her lids. She's so peaceful. And honestly, when she's asleep, she looks twelve. Vulnerable. Innocent. Pure.

It's when she opens her eyes that you see the woman.

I brush the tip of my nose against hers. She stirs, and I smile.

One of the stewards said she was the first on board today, arriving late this morning, but I hadn't seen her. I decided to get in a workout in the gym, but I can't wait for her to wake up anymore. I slowly lie down on her, my head resting on her chest as I tuck my arms under hers and hold her tight.

"Mmmm." She shifts under me and yawns. "You can't come at me with your seven-hundred-dollar perfume and expect me to keep this platonic, Rika. It's devastating."

I laugh. "Why are you sleeping?"

"Because some of us work nights." She stretches her arms above us and yawns again. "And we have a long one ahead of us."

Yes, we do. I close my eyes, her heartbeat filling my ears. I'd give anything not to have to leave this room, just stretch the minutes and make them last forever so Conclave never begins. She's my safe space.

"Need a hug?" she asks.

But before I can answer, her arms are wrapping around me and holding me, too.

"Nervous?" she asks.

I don't reply, though. If I don't make a big deal out of this, I can convince myself that my nerves are just overreacting. I soak up her warmth, her body heat under her cami soothing.

She strokes my hair. "You're too young for all this, you know?"

We all are. Yeah, I'm a twenty-two-year-old graduate student and mayor, and I've taken over a large portion of my inheritance, including businesses and properties, but we all have full plates. It seems the deeper we get, the more danger that arises.

Guilt nips at me. "And you're too good for all this," I tell her. Too good for all the tangles we bring into her life. "We love you, you know?" I still don't meet her eyes. "You're the breath that feeds the wolf."

I graze my thumbs over her arms, where my hands are tucked under her shoulders, and hold onto her, because she's the best of us. Still innocent. Still pure, no matter the ugliness that comes into her life. But no longer vulnerable. There's not a time when she isn't here for us, and I'm not sure if we'd be where we are without her.

I know I shouldn't seek refuge in her as much as I do, but there's so much going on, she seems to be the only one who realizes that I'm...

Weak.

When it comes down to it, I still feel like a kid playing at all of this.

I feel her swallow, and when she speaks, her voice is quiet. "Did I ever tell you about how I came to live at Delcour?"

No. And I hadn't pried much into her life except to discover she was thrown out of her house when she was seventeen, and she doesn't want to talk about her parents.

"I lived in the dorms my freshman year," she tells me, still stroking my hair in a steady rhythm. "Living off loans, a scholarship, and a part-time job working the beer tub at a dive club in Whitehall."

I listen. That would've only been months before we met, then.

"One night my roommate and I go out and party," she continues, "have lots of drinks, and come back to the dorm really lit and horny. She calls her boyfriend at Yale on her laptop. They always video chatted on her phone, so he and I never saw each other or met. I only knew he was a genius and twenty-two, a senior." She falls silent, and I wait. "We're talking and joking around, both of us kind of flirting with him and making him laugh—which wasn't easy to do, because he seemed a little sad. I can't pinpoint what it was, but it was there."

I remain still, waiting for her to go on.

"Anyway," she says, "we got on the subject of whether or not it's cheating if she sleeps with another girl. I look at him and her, and I...start unbuttoning her shirt." She lets out a small, quiet laugh like it seems so silly now. "I don't know when it changed from fooling around to full-on making out and undressing each other, but I looked over at his face on the computer, and his smile was gone. It was almost like he forgot how to breathe, you know? That's how entranced he was. He barely blinked as he watched us." Her voice drops to a whisper. "As he watched me."

I close my eyes, listening as she caresses my scalp.

"We fucked for him on my bed, Rika," she says.

I picture the scene she paints.

"The sex was a little boring—she was nervous and embarrassed," she explains, "so I had to take control—but I didn't want to stop, because I didn't want him to stop watching me. I thought he might touch himself and jerk off or something, but he didn't. He just watched and took everything in."

My mind goes back, and suddenly, I'm sixteen again, standing in the catacombs. I liked to watch, too. Or listen, because Michael blindfolded me that day.

"It was so hot." She goes back to rubbing my back, but I can tell she's lost in the memory. "It can be so much more exciting when you can't touch. I just wanted to never leave that night. Everything felt so fucking good."

Her chest rises under my head as she takes a deep breath and sighs.

"But things kind of went to shit between Aurora and me after that," she says. "She didn't say so, but I could tell she was ashamed. And it made me ashamed, because it felt natural at the time, and she was making it dirty. Like she was bullied into it, and I was weird for liking it. And she was also suspicious, and I didn't know why until she let it slip during an argument that he wanted to see us again. That he'd asked her if we would do it for him again."

Despite the disdain from her friend, a flutter hits my belly for Alex. I love her, and I can understand anyone who wants more of her. It's natural for Aurora to be jealous, but it's natural for Alex to like being desired.

"So, in a fit, she finally agreed," Alex tells me. "And I wanted to do it, too. I wanted more."

There's a pause before she continues.

"A half an hour later though, she walked out, they were broken up, and he was begging me not to stop."

Her voice is thick with pain. Did she stop? Would I have if it were Michael? Alex and this guy aren't together, so it either didn't end well, or it didn't begin at all.

"A week later," Alex nearly whispers, "they were back together and I was the campus slut."

I close my eyes again.

"A month later I'd lost my scholarship, and I hadn't seen or heard from him. Aurora and I were both kicked out of the dorms because of our fighting, and my boss at the club was introducing me to the first of many of his friends who would help me pay for my new apartment."

Jesus.

"Choices drive our lives," she goes on. "I sometimes think about where I'd be if I never wanted him to watch me so much. If I'd never started throwing fucks around to whoever paid for it, because if I could never hear him tell me how beautiful I was again, then I might not care what I did with my body or with who."

She tightens her arms around me.

"But then...I might never have become friends with you," she tells me. "My path with you and the guys might never have crossed, and I wouldn't have a family."

Her chest shakes under me, and my lungs swell. I feel her heavy breathing, and I know she's tearing up.

"I need Will back, Rika," she whispers.

I lift my head, resting my chin on her chest and seeing her eyes glisten.

She purses her lips to keep her emotions in check, but eventually, she explains, "I love you and Banks and Winter and the guys, but...Will gets it."

I stare at her, my heart breaking a little. Alex puts on a good show, but how easily it never occurred to me how much she was missing him. All the time Damon wasn't around, Alex was there for Will.

And we always looked at it like that, too. Alex is with Will. Alex is taking care of Will. Alex keeps Will company.

But none of that was really true. She hung onto him just as much as he hung onto her.

"He didn't deserve you," I tell her. "Your roommate's boyfriend."

She stares at me for a moment, looking a little pained, but then she lets out a sigh and forces a smile.

"Yeah, no one does," she jokes. "Not for less than five hundred an hour anyway."

I give her a pointed look at her sudden change in demeanor. "Alex..."

But she rolls us over and the next thing I know, her head is on my chest. "Rub my head now," she demands.

I pause there, aggravated she's changing the subject and putting up that façade again, but she holds me, dressed in her tank and underwear, and swings a long, naked leg over me. I let out a quiet laugh. *Hiding behind playfulness.* Will does that, too.

I start to rub her head, but then the cabin door opens, and we both look over, seeing Banks standing in the doorway.

She stops dead, her eyebrows nearly reaching her hairline as she catches us in our little, cuddly embrace.

Her mouth forms an O, and she starts to back out, closing the door.

"Get in here," I call out. "We're not doing anything."

For crying out loud.

She stops, a half-smile curling her lips and she comes back in, closing the door behind her.

"And get that constipated look off your face," Alex says.

Banks heads over to the bed, dressed in some workout clothes, same as me, but her hair is down. "Brat," she spits out.

Laying at my side, she joins me in giving Alex a scalp massage, except Banks' massage looks more like how you rub a dog's head, curling her fingers and lightly scratching.

"Stop that," Alex barks at her. "I hate you."

Banks and I both start to laugh. She has like fifty-eight dogs—okay, not that many, but a lot—so petting probably comes naturally to her.

I glance at Banks. "Mads okay?"

"Yup," she says. "At your mom's with the nannies, and hopefully Ivarsen by now, too."

Awesome. My mom is in baby heaven lately. Kai's mom, Vittoria, and her happily walking the streets of Thunder Bay and buying all the things for their grandsons. I'm surprised Ivarsen doesn't have a car already. *You know, just for when he's ready.*

"Where's Winter?" I ask her.

"Probably getting Damon-ed in the back seat of a car. She'll be here."

I snort. I think Winter lets him do anything he wants as much as he wants during this time, because she can't get pregnant if she's already pregnant.

"And Michael?" Alex chimes in.

"On his way," I reply.

Alex lifts up her head, and I stop rubbing her. "So..." She looks at Banks. "You and Kai." And then to me. "You and Michael. And Damon and Winter, and..."

"Misha and Ryen," I offer. They'll be here, because Misha is Will's cousin, so we have business he wants to be involved in.

"Misha and Ryen," she repeats absently. "And what am I supposed to do while everyone else takes 'breaks' tonight?"

She put "breaks" in air quotes as if she won't get any hot, little downtime, too.

Oh, who will she find to play with?

"There's a full crew," I assure her.

Her eyes go wide.

"And David and Lev will be boarding with Damon," Banks adds.

She gasps and then her face scrunches up into a delighted squeal. "It's like Christmas *and* my birthday together."

I ruffle her hair and roll her over, giving her quick pecks on the nose and cheek. "We got you. Don't worry."

She laughs, and Banks and I hop off the bed, heading for the door.

"Eight o'clock," I tell Alex, grabbing my AirPods and phone off the dresser.

She still lays in bed but gives me a thumbs up as she pulls her phone off the charger. I hesitate a moment, watching her and realizing that no matter how many people are in her life, there's something about her that always seems alone.

Banks and I leave, closing the door and walking down the corridor. She stops at her and Kai's cabin. "Eight o'clock," she says and pushes open her door.

I unlock my phone, already speed-dialing. "See you soon."

And I hold the phone to my ear, taking the stairs up to bridge deck.

The line rings twice before I hear Mr. Lyle's voice. "Ms. Fane," he says.

"Hi," I tell him. "Take this info, please."

There's silence, and then I hear him again. "Okay, ready."

"Alexandra Zoe Palmer, apartment 1608 at Delcour. Find her freshman year college roommate," I instruct. "And the woman's boyfriend that year, as well. Possibly a student at Yale at the time. I want the works by tomorrow."

"Got it."

"Thank you."

I hang up and step onto the bridge. I probably shouldn't pry in Alex's life, but I haven't decided if I'm going to yet. At least if I do, I'll be ready.

George Barris stands at the helm, going through his checklist and his first mate Samara Chen works at her station. I see faxes spitting out of the machine and I tear them off, reading them.

Pithom has a satellite weather system, but the captain likes to double up on precaution. Which is good.

I look over the weather reports and nod, satisfied. "You can take us out of the harbor," I tell him, starting to leave again. "Drop anchor about a mile out, and we'll wait for Mr. Crist."

"Yes, Ms. Fane."

I leave the papers for them and start to exit the bridge, but I stop, staring out the port-side window and seeing the stewards carrying a couple of suitcases on board. Someone else has arrived. A light layer of sweat cools my back and my stomach knots, but I know it's not Michael. He won't be in from Seattle for a couple hours.

Heading out, I descend the stairs to the owner's deck again, and make my way through the sitting area. I stop and pick a few pieces of prosciutto and cheese off the platter and stuff a slice of meat into my mouth.

I walk out to the sun deck, the dying light behind us, and see Damon standing at the edge of the boat looking down at the darkening water.

His eyebrows are pinched, and I cup my food in my hand, leaning against a column and watch him as I chew. The last time I stood where he stands, Will was in the water with a cinderblock tied to his ankle and Trevor was trying to kill me. Will and I were almost lost that night.

"Sometimes," Damon says, breaking the silence. "I let my mind wander enough, and it always comes back here."

He breathes hard, staring at the water as I stick a cube of cheese in my mouth.

"Except Michael doesn't catch him, and you never come up."

He turns and sits on the ledge, sliding his hands into his pockets and our eyes meet.

I see our mother in him now. A lot.

I didn't before. The way his eyes go big and round, and it takes a moment to be sure whether or not they're happily surprised or pissed off. The way he says what he wants and doesn't like to lie. The way they both hate being alone.

What an amazing thing time is. Three years ago, I thought I was going to die on this boat, him the last person I saw or talked to. I'd never been more scared.

Now, there's hardly a day that goes by where I don't speak to him or need him.

"You know..." I approach him.

He lifts his head, listening.

But I don't continue. I take a breath, let out a sigh, and...shoot out, shoving him hard in the chest.

His eyes go big, he flails, and the next thing I know, he's lost his footing and tips over the side of the yacht.

"Shit! Fuck!" rings out as he plummets.

His body hits the water ten feet down, a big splash as he disappears under the surface.

I stare down and pop another cold cut into my mouth, chewing. Did he land on his shoulder? How do you land on your frickin' shoulder?

He pops up through the surface, splashing and sputtering as he pushes his hair back over his head and glares up at me. I fight not to smile.

Water hangs on his eyelashes and lips, and I've never seen two more pissed-off eyebrows. "You little shit!" he bellows.

"Okay, yes, that was harsh. I admit it," I tell him, teasing. "But it was only fair. I almost died that night, Damon."

"Get your ass in here, and I'll show you what death looks like!"

"Are you crazy?" I pick up another piece of cheese. "That water's really cold."

He growls and swims for the back of the boat, and I finally let myself laugh as I grab a towel for him. He looks so vulnerable.

Walking down the stairs, I watch as he hops up onto the back of the yacht and stands up, his white dress shirt and black pants sticking to his body.

But his hair looks good.

I bite back my smile and hold out the towel.

"Piss off."

But he snatches it from my hand anyway.

What a baby. I guess some people can only dish it out.

"You know that guilt I was feeling a minute ago?" he blurts out. "It's all gone now."

"Good." I nod once. "We have bigger things to deal with tonight anyway."

He seethes, drying off his hair and face and kicking off his shoes.

"Everyone in?" I hear someone call. "We're ready to shove off."

I look up at the captain, standing up on the bridge deck.

I give him a wave. "We're ready."

Damon and I climb the stairs again and walk across the sun deck as the engines start purring a little louder.

42

"Is Michael here?" he asks.

"He's coming." I dump out the rest of my uneaten food and grab a bottle of water. "I wish everyone would stop asking me that."

I move around the bar, ready to head to my cabin to shower, but Damon grabs my arm.

I stop, meeting his dark eyes.

"Everything on the table tonight," he commands. "Everything."

My heart skips a beat, and my muscles, relaxed a moment ago, start to tighten and strain again.

But I nod in agreement. "I know."

As the yacht moves out into the darkening Atlantic and the stars light the night sky, nothing but Damon's words play in my mind over the next two hours. *Everything on the table.* I shower, I dress, and I barely have the stomach to think about anything else, other than what's going to happen in the next hour. Or the next four hours.

Or tomorrow.

Everything hinges on tonight.

I put on my lipstick, and the faint sound of propellers echo in the distance as dread sits on my lungs, making it hard to breathe. I look up at my ceiling, turning my eyes toward the sound of the helicopter above descending onto the yacht.

Michael is here.

• • •

The bells chime eight, all the clocks in the cabins singing the hour, as well as a faint *dong* of the tower clock in the wine room carrying through the corridors of the yacht.

Michael didn't come to find me when he arrived. I leave my room, taking my phone, silent of any texts or calls I thought he'd send when I wasn't in our cabin. It's for the best, though. It's why I decided to get ready in another part of the boat, other than the place we share. I don't want to see him until I go in there. I'll lose my nerve.

Ryen, Misha's girlfriend, steps through their door, followed closely by him, and she looks over at me coming her way.

I smile, unable to stop my eyes from trailing down her body. She wears a tight black dress, falling about mid-thigh, with black heels that make me feel a little short. Misha turns to me, wearing a tailored black suit, minus the tie, and no matter what Damon says about his tattoos, they really do go with everything.

We're all in black, and I almost laugh. I'm glad it's understood that tonight is for a power color.

He holds out his hand, waving me by. "Lead the way," he says.

I walk ahead, feeling them follow me. Alex's door opens as I pass by, and I see her fall in with Misha and Ryen as the four of us head toward the bow, under the sun deck and deeper into the ship.

Glass walls shimmer with the firelight from the sconces, and I turn into an open doorway, seeing a large room spread before me as Kai, Winter, Banks, and Damon all stand around. Floor-to-ceiling windows decorate the far wall ahead, and the sea spreads before us as the engines whir again. Michael gazes out at the night, his back to me.

I drift slowly into the room as Misha, Ryen, and Alex walk past me, but I can't take my eyes off him. My insides melt, and after all the years of wanting him and loving him,

I'm still sixteen with a crush from afar. Loving someone so much it hurts.

The stewards finish setting out food and drinks on the buffet table, pulling a couple bottles of red off the racks on the walls and opening them for us. As soon as they leave, the doors close, and everyone drifts to the large, round table, finding their seats.

Michael turns and our eyes lock. His hazel gaze holds me frozen, and it's hard to breathe, because I see it in his eyes. I always see it.

The love. The need. The longing.

But now, it's different. There's a hesitance there now, too. Like he's unsure of what to do with me.

His beautiful eyes glide down my body, taking in my long, thin, black gown with a plunging neckline and cutouts on the back and sides, damn-near to my ass. A leather belt wraps around my waist and naked back to hold the dress to my body. I take a step forward, my leg popping out of the slit all the way up to my hip, and I know what he sees. Or doesn't see underneath my dress.

His jaw clenches, and his gaze darts up to me again, a small fire blazing behind his eyes. I want to take pleasure in it. Taunting him.

But I simply love it. I love us.

I take the seat closest to me as Kai, Banks, and Alex go to my right and Misha, Ryen, Damon, and Winter sit to my left. Michael takes the last remaining seat, across the table, directly opposite of me.

But then he quickly rises again. "Before we begin…"

We watch as he opens a shiny black box on the table and pulls out several smaller black cases. He slides one each to Damon, Kai, and Misha, and takes one himself, circling the table toward me.

"When Will comes back," he says to everyone, "we'll figure out something for the men, but...every family has their heirlooms."

He stops at my side, meeting my eyes. Boxes flip open as everyone busies themselves, looking to see what it is, while every nerve under my skin fires at his attention. He opens the box, setting it down on the table and removes the item inside.

"So, let these be our first," he adds, holding up an ornate black necklace with a pendant in the center.

"What is it?" I hear Winter ask as Damon pulls hers out of the box.

"It's a necklace," he says.

"It's a collar," Banks spits out.

Michael and I share a smile at her jab.

But it's beautiful. Regal. Thin, black chains weave together, dotted by small black jewels, and in the center sits an oval broach. Michael drapes the necklace around me as Kai and Damon put theirs on Banks and Winter.

"It has a white pendant," Damon explains to Winter. "With a skull. The skull has antlers above a bed of grass where a snake lies."

"The skull represents our true faces." Michael fastens the clasp at the back of my neck, the necklace only falling as far as my collar bone. "What comes out of us when we put on our masks."

"The call of the void," Damon whispers to Winter.

Michael continues, "The antlers represent a deer which means watchfulness, being in touch with your inner child, innocence, and vigilance. The snake means rebirth and transformation."

I touch the broach with my fingers. "And fertility," I add as an afterthought.

Michael holds my gaze for a moment and then turns away, heading back around the table.

He takes another box and sets it down next to Alex, opening it up.

But she stops him. "I want Will to put it on me."

He nods and closes the box again.

Standing at his place at the table, he looks over at Misha and Ryen, who just stare at the item still tucked inside its box.

"It belongs to the family," he tells her. "If you forfeit it, you forfeit it to us or no one. Do you understand?"

She looks between him and Misha at her side, nodding nervously. "I appreciate the gesture," she says, glancing back at Misha. "We have some things to think about."

Misha doesn't say anything, and I absolutely understand their reluctance. I don't know Ryen well, but this isn't him. Misha likes freedom, not answering to anyone but her, and I've never known him to be in a club other than his band. Too many people interfering with his privacy would paralyze him. It's not who he is.

And quite frankly, they don't have a history with us. The rest of us are here, because we wouldn't be anywhere else. Misha is here for Will and only Will.

Michael takes his seat and swipes his fingers across his phone, setting it in the middle of the table to record the minutes. "All right, considering our agenda, let's first tackle the—"

"I want to kill your father," I say, cutting him off.

Damon chokes on his vodka rocks. Every eye at the table turns to me, and Michael silently stares as my words hang in the air.

I know it was abrupt, but I need to set the pace tonight. Or I'll lose control.

"I won't," I add. "I just want to. I wanted you to know that."

Michael sits there, playing with the Montblanc in front of him as everyone watches on silently, but he doesn't blink, and neither do I.

"And I want to marry you," he tells me. "Is this why you're dragging your feet? My father?"

I falter. One has nothing to do with the other. "That's a private matter."

"You don't talk even when we are in private. The only time things are good lately is when we're fucking."

Damon shoves his chair back, making Banks and Ryen jump, and rises, scowling at Michael.

But Michael is already on it, not bothering to get out of his seat as he glares up at Damon. "I was there when she was five and eight and thirteen, so you remember where you and she started the next time you want to imply you have any more responsibility or love for her than I do," he bites out. "My woman. Sit down."

I'm simultaneously hit with flutters over Michael's words and appreciation for Damon's protectiveness. As much it hurt, though, Michael was right. Things are okay but only great when we're in bed lately.

Damon hesitates, but finally sits, still seething, and I look back at Michael.

He turns his gaze back on me. "This was your fantastic idea," he says. "So out with it. You resent me for not avenging you. My father killed yours." And then he gazes around the table, leaning back in his chair. "Is that how you all see it? I haven't defended her?"

But before they can chime in, I tell him, "I don't resent you. I love you." I am a little hurt by his lack of urgency, but I understand the position he's in. "And I'll die your wife or I'll die no one's."

There. Happy now?

He stares at me, hopefully understanding there's no doubt in my love or devotion.

He clears his throat. "The only living witness I could manage to locate was murdered last year." He tosses a look at Damon, referring to Gabriel's demise. "And even if I could find more, I can't put my mother through the humiliation." He drops his eyes, pausing. "I know what your father's death did to your mother, Rika. What you're asking is only fair. I know that." His eyes raise to mine again, pained. "But I killed her son, Rika. I can't...kill her..."

He falls silent, but he doesn't need to finish the sentence.

I know. Even if his father "quietly disappeared," Michael wouldn't lie to her. She'd find out, and she'd be hurt by him. She might even start to fear him.

"I'll do it," Damon chimes in.

Michael nods absently. "I know you will, but I'm not going to let you. You have things to live for now. Don't put yourself at unnecessary risk." He sighs, sitting back again. "We can't slaughter every problem anyway."

No, we can't. We're not criminals, and I have to constantly remind myself of that. We don't break laws for personal gain. We do it for fun.

We don't have to kill him, but things can't stay the same, either. "I want him gone. Out of Thunder Bay," I tell Michael. "And out of Meridian City."

"We can't buy him out," he replies.

"We won't have to," Banks interjects.

Everyone stops, turning to her. The skin of her bare shoulders glowing in the candlelight, and I sit up in my chair, meeting her eyes.

"He'll give everything to us," she says.

I hold back my smile. My favorite thing about Banks is that she proudly refrains from bringing anything to the table unless it's a solution. I'm listening.

She turns to Michael. "Killing Schraeder Fane isn't all your father is guilty of, to be sure. We'll find something and use it to persuade him."

"Persuade him to do what?"

"Seek life elsewhere," she replies sarcastically.

Michael shakes his head. "He still won't leave quietly."

"Then we'll take care of it," Kai says, losing patience. "We're only doing what's necessary, Michael. We have kids to think about. Rika's right. He can't stay."

It takes a moment, but Michael finally looks up at me, and I know what's going through his head. Yes, his father is dangerous. Yes, he's hurt people immeasurably.

But couldn't we say the same things about ourselves? We've hurt each other. We've killed.

The difference between us and Evans Crist, though, is that he acted out of greed and a lust for power. We've always acted out of what we thought was service to our family. Our true family. Evans barely acts with consideration for his wife and Michael. He won't care about the rest of us. I don't want Mads and Ivar anywhere near him.

Slowly, Michael nods.

"And I don't want his name," I add.

He stills, his eyes slowly rising to meet mine.

I know he probably feels targeted so far in this meeting, but I need it out, and better sooner than later. I'm not changing my name when we marry.

His chest rises and falls slow and steady, but I can tell he's fucking pissed. "I want you to have the same last name as your children."

"I will."

My heart pounds, because I don't want to hurt him, but I can't bend on this. It's something I've thought a lot about. Why should I have to change my name? Who made that rule anyway? My father was a good man who left no sons to carry on the name. He deserves this.

My last words hang in the air as no one breathes at the table, and Michael stares at me, the growing anger playing behind his eyes. I know I'm asking a lot. He was born with a name he thought he'd carry his entire life. He doesn't have to change his.

But I'm not changing mine. Michael and I are locked, but neither of us says more, probably because we don't know what to say. He either wants to yell and doesn't want to do it here, or he wants to throttle me.

"Al...right," Kai stammers, and I know he's glancing between Michael and me. "We'll... come back to that, then."

Everyone shifts around the table, but Michael won't look away first, so I do. I'll let him have that.

"Will..." Kai says, moving onto the next subject. "What do we know?"

Misha sits up. "The last text I got from him was months—"

"Forget texts," Kai states, looking around the table. "When was the last time we had a visual on him?"

"Thirteen months."

We turn to Damon, his whisper hanging in the air as he rolls an unlit cigarette between his fingers.

"And twelve days," Alex adds. "He video called."

Thirteen months. I blink long and hard. *Thirteen fucking months.*

"And we can rule out he's not dead, because his parents aren't worried," I tell them.

Misha pulls something out of his breast pocket and unfolds it, setting it down on the table. Damon immediately snatches it.

"What's this?" he asks, inspecting the sheet.

"A list of males from wealthy and prominent families who have fallen off the grid and reappeared over the past thirty years," Misha explains.

Damon scoffs, flinging the paper over to Michael. "We usually deal in digital files here in the twenty-first century."

Michael takes the paper, scanning it.

"And what good is interviewing a bunch of middle-aged dudes going to do?" Damon continues. "A. They won't talk. No one talks about Blackchurch. And B. The location changes. Even if they did talk, they wouldn't know where it was anymore."

"Maybe the location doesn't change," Misha argues. "Maybe that's part of the story they tell us. And maybe Warner... Stratford... Walmart Cunningham III can give us a lead. Something useful. Unless you have a better idea?"

"His grandfather," Winter chimes in. "He's the one who probably put him there to begin with, right?"

Michael turns to Alex, plotting the next step. "Can you get in?"

She laughs under her breath. "I don't know why you think these men divulge state secrets to their whores."

"Because it's worked before." Damon grins, teasing her. "You don't give yourself enough credit."

But I sit up. "No."

They all look at me.

"We're not using Alex like that," I explain.

At some point, she'll finish her graduate degree, get a new job, and what will we do then when we can't pimp her out? I'm not sending her to that old man.

"Besides," I go on. "Men like him don't handle the details themselves anyway."

"His assistant, then," Kai says. "Jack Munro. He'll know everything."

"And if he won't talk?" Misha retorts.

"I'm sure information is more forthcoming when you want to put someone in there instead of take them out," Alex mumbles.

The table falls silent, but I see a slight smile curl Michael's lips.

"What?" I ask.

He quickly hides his smile and shrugs. "Nothing."

But I watch him for a moment. He's thinking something.

Alex draws in a breath. "I'll ingratiate myself to Senator Grayson's assistant as soon as Conclave concludes." And she meets my gaze before I can say anything. "I'm doing it, Rika."

I swallow my argument, not happy putting her into the position, but it's Will, and I know she'll do whatever it takes at this point.

Winter sets her hand on the table. "And if we find Blackchurch, and he's there, how do we get him out?"

"We need to know what kind of fortress we're dealing with first," Banks tells her. "If the stories are true, they'll have free run of the house and grounds. If we're able to get to them, then they're also able to get to us."

The table falls silent as Banks looks around at each of us.

"There's a reason Blackchurch is like that," she continues. "Why it's not simply a luxury spa with locked cages and guards. Why they're left alone as if they're dogs thrown into a pit to eat or be eaten."

Images flash in my mind of what she's describing, and how, at this moment, Will could be sitting in that place. My head falls.

"They've burned their bridges and decided not to be part of a family," Banks goes on, "so now they'll learn their place in the natural order."

The natural order. Tough love on crack. They have their needs provided for. Food, shelter, medical attention, if needed... But otherwise, they're completely alone and...at each other's mercy.

"They will have resorted to base instinct," Banks tells us. "Their lives are about survival now. The rest of the world does not exist anymore. They're a system of their own with rules and laws..." She pauses. "And consequences."

She might know more about Blackchurch since Gabriel considered sending Damon, or she might just know what happens to dogs in cages. Either way, I know everything she says is true.

"They're hoarding food," she says, "each one of them fighting for their share. They're forming alliances to protect each other, and they will have made weapons with whatever's laying around."

My chest constricts.

"There will be an alpha," she continues, "and Will... will not be it."

None of us speak as, I'm sure, everyone's mind is going to the same place as mine. Imagining Will and what he's possibly living through right now. Those men are not his friends. Will isn't strong by himself.

He isn't Michael. He isn't Kai.

"I'm going to be sick," Winter chokes out, tears filling her eyes as she rises from her seat.

Damon gets up, takes her hand, and they both leave the room.

The door closes again.

"How did we let this go for so long?" Kai breathes out.

"We fucked up," Misha says, his eyes now more worried than ever.

But Ryen chimes in. "Will's okay."

Alex looks over at her, a tear falling down her face. "How do you know that?"

"Because he has an advantage over those other prisoners," she tells us. "He's been in prison already. He's done this before."

I tuck my lips between my teeth and close my eyes, trying to calm myself. She's right. I swallow and try to unknot my fucking stomach. If Will is there, he's alive.

"Jack Munro," Michael says, looking at Alex. "You make contact, and we want to hear from you as soon as it's over." And then he repeats, "As **soon** as it's over."

She nods.

"Let's take a break, then," he tells us.

The room suddenly feels too tight, and I push my chair back as everyone rises from theirs. I need some air.

The food on the table sits uneaten as everyone drifts out the door to stretch their legs. I turn to leave, but someone grabs my hand, stopping me.

I look up at Michael, both of us silent as the room slowly empties.

"Say my name," he whispers.

The vein in my neck throbs.

"Michael," I say.

"That's not how you say it." He inches closer, taking my face in his hand. "How you've always said it."

I want to look away, because I can feel the tears at the back of my throat. I want to tell him. I want to get rid of this pain and fear, but... Our future looks perfect. I'm about to change it.

And I can't.

We're in love. Right now, in this moment. Things change in seconds, and I can't.

"Where did you go?" He searches my eyes. "Where are you right now?"

I feel my chin tremble.

"There's something else you're not telling me."

I open my mouth to say it. Or kiss him or anything, but I...

I have all night. I can't yet.

Pulling away from him, I turn on my heel and charge out of the room.

"Rika!" he barks.

But I don't stop. I swipe the tear off my cheek just as it falls and make my way out toward the sun deck, passing through the lounge area where everyone is congregating on the couches with a drink.

I stop at the edge, peering out over the black ocean, a white beam of moonlight spreading into the horizon. The wind blows through my dress, the chilly air doing nothing to soothe my nerves.

Just let me make love to him one more time before I fuck everything up.

"How far out are we going?" someone suddenly asks.

I blink away my tears, looking over my shoulder at Ryen.

"The boat's been moving for a few hours now," she points out, laughing a little. "We must be far enough out. No one is escaping to shore at this point."

I turn back around, fixing my eyes on the sea. "I told them not to stop until they hear from me," I tell her. "Or we hit land."

"The next land is Ireland," Misha says.

I force a smirk. "Then we better work fast."

Actually, Misha and Ryen can probably sit the rest of the night out. Their business is done, and they certainly won't need to hear the rest of what goes on. The Cove. Damon's inheritance. His plans to put Banks in D.C., which he thinks I don't know about, but really, it makes perfect sense.

Will's grandfather spends most of his career staying in power, and while Damon's motivation isn't entirely selfless, Banks would be suited for it. Once she finishes her degree, he'll convince her to run for state legislature until she's thirty and old enough to run for Senate. Everyone perfectly positioned to make the world how we want it to be and connected enough to keep making money. It's shady as hell, but she won't be bad in that office. Not bad at all.

If she goes for it, that is. Unfortunately, I foresee a huge fight first.

I turn around, seeing Damon enter the lounge, and I grip the railing behind me. "How's Winter?"

"She's okay," he assures, carrying a box to the table. "Just freshening up."

He plops down at the table, across from Misha and Ryen, and turns his attention to them.

"Babysoft," he teases and dumps a box on the table in front of Ryen.

"What is this?" she asks, opening it up.

She reaches in and pulls out an ornate, black eye mask made of metal with black ribbons to secure it around her head. The design allows for her skin to peek through the gaps and has exotic holes for the eyes. It's more a masquerade-type mask than what we wear. It's beautiful, though.

"It's the girl who comes out when you and Misha are alone," Damon explains. "It's for when it's dark and private, and he wants to do fun things with you."

Misha takes it out of her hand and sticks it back in the box. "No."

Damon laughs, amused but not shocked. Or fazed.

"Just let her try it on." He pushes the box back to Ryen and looks at her. "Later. When you're alone. See if you like what comes out." And then he turns his gaze back to Misha standing up. "See if she hears it. Maybe you'll hear it, too."

They don't ask what he means, but I know. *L'appel du vide*. Winter's philosophy of who we are and what brings us together. Maybe Misha and Ryen are more like us than we thought. Maybe everyone is. Given the chance.

But Misha just sighs and pushes his chair back, getting up. "I need to be drunk to deal with you." He walks to the bar.

Damon follows, making himself a drink, but he doesn't bug Misha further. I glance at the doorway, noticing Michael hasn't followed us. He's probably ready to wring my neck.

I cross the lounge and step into the head, closing the door. But it catches, and I look up, seeing Kai slip in behind me and quickly shut the door.

My eyes immediately sting, and I didn't realize how hard I'm holding back until I'm alone with him. He approaches me in the quiet, secluded little space in front of the sink and takes my face in his hands.

He looks at me, and my eyes water.

"I know," I whisper. "I know."

"You're torturing both of you," he says. "Tell him."

My chest shakes, and I try to look away, but he doesn't let me. He holds my face in place.

"It has to be in private," I tell him. "He'll be angrier if I put him on the spot in front of everyone."

"He won't be angry."

He'll be in a terrible position, though. One where he'll be between a rock and a hard spot, and I'd be asking him to make a choice where both options leave him giving up something he wants.

I need to make the choice for him. I always knew that.

I let my head drop, slowly falling forward into Kai's chest. "It would kill me to see him with another woman," I whisper. "What if he marries someone else, and I have to live in Thunder Bay and see them?"

I start to cry, feeling his arms circle around me, and I break down, the dread and anticipation sitting in my stomach and making me sick.

Kai whispers against my hair. "Shhhh..."

But the door suddenly swings open, and we pop our heads up. Michael stands there, and the look on his face makes my stomach sink. He bares his teeth, grabs Kai by the jacket, and hauls him out of the bathroom.

I gasp as he throws his friend back into the lounge, Kai crashes into the table, the vase on top sliding off and breaking on the floor. Ryen yelps, scurrying out of her seat and out of the way.

Michael charges over to Kai, grabbing him again and fisting his lapels.

"Whoa, whoa, stop!" Kai growls.

"Michael, stop!" I yell.

He shakes Kai, shouting in his face. "What the hell were you doing?"

"We were just talking!" Kai tells him.

Damon stands frozen, watching but ready, while Misha, Ryen, and Banks look on with worried stares at the scene.

Michael leans in, speaking low in Kai's face. "You don't touch her."

"It wasn't like that," Kai argues.

"Then what was it like?"

This came from Banks, and I turn my eyes on her, her doubt stinging.

Michael throws Kai off, breathing hard, and Kai looks at Banks, fixing his suit and looking exasperated.

"Just hold up, okay?" he tells everyone. He's not sure what to say to explain himself to his wife and protect me at the same time. I put him in that position.

I step forward. "Michael..."

"Fuck you, Rika," he says, cutting me off.

He stands up straight, turning his attention on me, and I tense.

"Fuck your power, your schedule, your assistant," he tells me, "your fucking little entourage everywhere you go, your plans, and your chess games. I gave you too much power."

I can't move. Slowly, the bricks of every moment we built together start to shake, and I don't know if I'm more shocked by his sudden disdain, or the fact that he actually thought Kai and I were...

"And you know," he goes on, "I wanted this. I wanted you to own it. I didn't want another version of my mother. Silent, docile, living separate lives. I wanted my other half." He looks at me, and I don't see love anymore. Just hurt. "And I got it," he says sadly. "When I look in the mirror, all I see is your face. I can't tell the difference anymore." He hesitates and gestures to Kai and Damon. "I'm all about you, and you...? You talk to them, instead of me."

"Well, you are gone a lot," Damon points outs.

Michael holds my eyes for only a moment before he hauls off and hits Damon, slamming his fist right across his face.

"Michael!" I shout.

Damon grunts, falling onto the sofa, but shoots back off quickly, glaring and charging ahead.

But Kai holds him back, stopping him.

Michael forgets his attack and looks at me. "I'm retiring after next season," he tells me. "Will you talk to me, then?"

Retiring? I shake my head. "You're twenty-five. You still have years if you don't get injured."

"It's time to concentrate on other things. The Cove, our family..."

"We can't move on the Cove until we get Will home," Damon commands.

"Will won't stop it from happening," Michael replies, planting his hands and leaning on the table. "It's time to level the property and begin."

"Whoa, whoa, the Cove?" Misha steps forward. "You're not tearing it down!"

But Michael slams the table with his fists, shutting everyone up. We all stand silent as he dips his head, staring at the table.

I inch forward. This is my fault, not theirs.

Finally, he looks up at me, his voice softer. "I feel less than you," he says. "Like..."

"Like you have nothing to teach me anymore," I finish for him.

He doesn't respond, so I know I'm right. He's intimidated that I have more going on than just him.

"I'm not your pet," I tell him.

I was once, but not anymore.

"Why?" he asks.

Why? He's asking why I won't be his pet? Seriously?

He rises and walks around the table, approaching me.

"Because..." I say. "Because I need to be more. I need to be...useful."

"Why?"

I want to laugh, not out of amusement but anger. I'm not a trophy. I'm not something to play with or program.

"Because I need you to see what I can do," I tell him. I need to prove myself.

"Why?" He inches closer.

I open my mouth, but I can't find my words. I know what he's doing, and the tears start to fill my eyes. I just need to say it.

"Because I don't want you to be disappointed in me," I whisper. "Because you'll be disappointed."

He stands in front of me, only a few inches between us. "Why?"

"Because I can't...I..." I stutter, swallowing the lump in my throat. "I can't have children." I close my eyes, silently starting to cry as the words leave my mouth. "I can't give us a family."

He stands there, not coming any closer, and while my heart is breaking at the life we can't have, a weight lifts off my shoulders. I didn't want to do this in front of everyone, because Michael will be the gentleman and assure me it's okay. We'll adopt. We'll hire a surrogate. We'll be fine.

But months down the road, he'll start to understand it's not that simple. He'll resent the life he can't have, and I'll feel like I'm keeping him from something better.

"My cycles have always been long, but..." I continue, "I'm not ovulating regularly. The doctor says it's unlikely."

"But not impossible," Banks clarifies, approaching me. "Have you tried other doctors?"

"Yes."

Damon steps forward. "Well, once you get off birth control—"

"I've been off for two years," I tell him. "And I haven't had a period in over one."

"A year," Michael says, more to himself. "About how long you've been carrying this around, right?"

But it comes out sounding like an accusation before he turns his eyes on Kai. "Why don't you seem surprised?" he asks him.

But Kai just looks away. He's the only one who knew, and I understand what Michael is feeling. But I didn't confide in Kai. He just found out.

He went through the whole pep talk with me. *Michael loves you. You have options. People make it work every day. Lots of kids need good homes.* But people also break up over these things. Every day. People want children of their own. They want to make children with the man or woman they love. I never thought something like this would get in my way, but I'm scared. It's easy to say I'm valuable. He loves me for me, and if my body can't do this, it can't be all he needs from me. I'm worth plenty, even if I can't give him our children, right? This isn't my fault. I haven't failed.

But believing those words and feeling them is more difficult. What if he tries but he decides this is just too hard? What if I can never accept that I can't do this for him?

I can't look at him as I whisper, "We won't have any children together, Michael."

That's as plain as I can put it. He needs to know the likelihood is slim.

I wait for him to not be angry. To give some sign that this isn't the end of the world, and he still loves me more than anything, but...

He turns and walks away.

He leaves the room, leaving me standing there with tears on my face. Emptiness aches in my body everywhere. He hates me. God, he hates me. I can't breathe.

"You knew?" I hear Banks ask.

"I found out," Kai tells her. "It was an accident."

I sniffle, my hands shaking. Oh, my God. He left. He walked out.

I close my eyes again.

"We're killing him," Damon growls, and he's probably talking to Kai. "Right now."

Banks, Ryen, and Alex step over, trying to hold me, but I shake them off gently. "It's okay. I'm okay." I wipe my eyes and move forward. "Excuse me, please."

And I hurry out of the room, covering my mouth with my hand as I go, so they can't hear the sobs.

• • •

Fuck you, Rika.

Something constricts my throat, and I startle awake, unsure if it was a noise or the sudden quiet that jostles me.

The engines have stopped. I lift my head and look around the dark room, seeing it's still empty and the bed untouched. What time is it?

I'm still curled up in the chair in Michael's and my cabin, having buried myself in it when I finally found the courage to step inside.

But he wasn't here when I came in.

Setting my feet on the floor, I wipe my eyes and stand up, looking around again. It's still dark outside. I glance at the clock on the dresser, the little bells chiming midnight.

It's been three hours since the fight. Where is he? Why have we stopped?

Of course, I have no interest in going to Ireland right now anyway, so I'm kind of glad.

Leaving my heels next to the chair, I pick up the hem of my dress, so I don't trip, and walk barefoot to the door. Opening it, I peer outside into the corridor.

"Michael?" I call.

Then, I listen.

But nothing. No noise coming from the other cabins. No music. No movement or conversation.

Stepping out of the room, I walk, swiping my fingers under my eyes to tidy up the eyeliner as I go. After the argument, I'd drifted to the bow to cool off and try to get my head straight. I'd put myself through every mental argument I could over the past several months leading up to this conversation, and not only did I completely blow it, but I expected everything from him except the one thing I got. Silence.

He just walked away like I was nothing. I was right to worry, after all, it seems.

Even if he were okay with it, I don't know if I would be. He'll go on, watching his friends have their babies, but it won't be like that for us, and I hate that. I'd hate doing that to him.

I shake my head, taking breaths to calm myself. I don't want to lose him.

After a while, I'd decided to go have it out privately, but when I went to the cabin, he wasn't there. I curled up on the chair to wait and drifted off.

I hear splashes and look over the side of the boat and see people jumping into the water down at the stern.

Ryen and Banks swim back to the boat, while Kai and Misha jump in over their heads. They all laugh, blowing off steam while they can. Conclave still goes on, whether we're in that room or not, I guess. It's just Michael and me for now, though.

I take the stairs to the bridge. "Hello?"

"Hello?"

"Mr. Barris?" I say, stepping into the room.

We still face east, but he's stopped the boat for now.

"Ms. Fane." He rises from his chair. "Everything okay?"

I rub my arms, extra aware of my lack of under-clothes now. "Have you seen Mr. Crist?"

"Not for a while, no."

I nod absently. Well, he couldn't have gone far, at least.

I turn to leave but stop, noticing he's been in the bridge all day.

"Where is Ms. Chen?" I ask. He should be getting to sleep soon.

He stares at me for a moment and then says, "I dismissed her for the evening a while ago."

But then he looks away, and something unnerves me. Like he didn't want to tell me that.

I look after him for a moment, watching him busy himself with something silly, and finally, I decide to leave. What's wrong with dismissing her for the night? Why would he look uncomfortable telling me that?

Heading back to the owner's deck, I slowly walk down the corridor, lightly knocking on rooms I know are unoccupied. He could be sleeping it off somewhere else to avoid me. I search the galley, the dining area, the lounge, and the wine room. There's no one in the steam room; but the farther I go, the louder my heart beats in my ears, because if I haven't found him yet, then he's somewhere he doesn't want to be found.

A thought occurs to me and my stomach rolls with nausea. Did Michael ask for Ms. Chen to be dismissed from the bridge early? Is that why Barris looked at me so weird?

The boat rocks under my feet, and I stop for a moment, steadying myself.

It's not the boat. I'm dizzy.

Michael...

I swallow. No, he wouldn't do that.

I descend the last set of stairs, the machines and engines humming quietly as the low lights glow across the red floors. I tread in the shadows, around giant cylinders, afraid to look in the nooks and small spaces, but this place—in the bowels of the yacht—is the only place left to search.

Maybe he's with Damon and Winter. Maybe he took the speedboat back to shore?

A flash goes off ahead, and I look up, catching movement somewhere behind the tanks.

Slowly, I head that way.

Another flash goes off, and I hear a shuffle as I peer between two large white tanks, two more flashes going off. It's a camera.

A woman with long, dark hair sits on top of a table, its legs nailed to the floor and her naked body in full view of whoever takes her picture. Her face is covered behind her hair, but I know who it is. It's too long to be Banks and too dark to be Alex.

Samara Chen.

I watch as our first mate leans back on her hands, one foot propped up on the table and one leg dangling, as someone takes her picture over and over again. I close my eyes for a moment. I want to see who it is, but I'm pretty sure I already know.

I open my eyes, watching Samara slip her fingers between her legs, her hair falling behind her shoulders, so I can see her eyes now, eye-fucking the camera in front of her as she rubs herself in circles. The long lines of her torso, the smooth skin of her hips and back, her full, beautiful breasts...

An image of Michael fucking her on that table flashes in my mind, and my stomach twists again and again like a rubber band, and I clench my fists.

But as I slowly step to the side, my heart pounding so hard it hurts as I look around the tank, I see it's not Michael taking her picture.

Alex has changed into a casual pair of gray lounge pants and white V-neck T-shirt. She holds a camera in her hands, cocking her head and watching as Ms. Chen props both legs up on the table, spreading wide for Alex's view.

I release the breath I'd been holding.

But then, out of the corner of my eye, I spot movement. Lev enters from somewhere he'd been standing beyond my line of sight and walks over to the table, shoving Samara down hard.

She whimpers, and I suck in a breath. Alex holds his eyes for a moment, and then he dives down, eating the girl's pussy.

He licks and sucks, nibbles and rubs, her body arching off the table as he goes at her without pause. She moans, and he wraps his hand around her thigh, holding her in place as Alex continues photographing them.

I should leave. I step back but run into something hard, and I pause, the hair on my arms standing up straight. A long arm with long fingers reaches around me, and I spot the same beautiful vein in his hand bulging as he grips his bottle of Kirin, handing it to me.

A flutter hits my heart, and I'm sixteen again, back at St. Killian's. I take the beer, looking up at the scene in front of us as he remains behind me. I take a swig, the bitter bubbles popping on my tongue.

Lev licks her slow but steady, rubbing his tongue around her clit and kneading her breasts. She moans, her hips rolling into his mouth, hungry for more. Another flash goes off as we watch them, silently tucked away and hidden.

"I love you," I say, clutching the bottle.

I'm glad when he doesn't respond, because I need to say this now that we're alone.

"What's my worth if I keep you from having the one thing most people really want?" I pause, staring at the scene but barely paying attention. "I couldn't lose you, Michael."

I take another sip, remembering that first taste all those years ago.

"I couldn't lose you, but I couldn't marry you, either," I tell him. "Not under a lie." I draw in a deep breath despite the tears lodged in my throat. "I just wanted to be able to love you as long as possible, because I don't want you to give up your chance to have children, and I don't know if I can cope not being able to give them to you. I feel like shit. All the time. I can't stomach the thought of you having a family with anyone else, but I don't want to make you unhappy, either."

I'm hurting.

He's still silent, and I don't know if I've explained myself or if I make any sense.

He takes the bottle from my hand, and I hear the liquid slosh as he tips the bottle back for a drink. I wait, because everything hinges on hearing his voice.

"I knew you were in my truck that day," he says in a low voice.

I blink. What?

"I saw the backdoor open in the rearview mirror," he explains. "And then I saw it close."

In his truck...?

And then it hits me. Devil's Night so long ago when I snuck into his truck to follow him and his friends. The same one where he let me try his beer for the first time.

"You weren't old enough for everything," he continues, "but you were old enough for some things, and I couldn't wait anymore. It was always there. Since we were kids."

Ms. Chen's moans and whimpers fill the engine room as she holds Lev's mouth to her pussy, their pace and breathing growing stronger and faster.

"Sometimes, I thought I wanted to touch you," Michael whispers, and I feel it on the top of my hair. "Other times, I thought I wanted to kill you. I didn't know if it was love or hate, but I knew it would change my life."

"Slower, Lev," Alex tells him, snapping a photo.

But he argues. "Come on, she tastes so good."

"Like this." Alex leans in, kissing Ms. Chen and Lev follows her lead, both of them devouring the young woman.

"Oh, my God," Chen pants, arching her back off the table.

I close my eyes, the memory of those same sounds coming back to me. "And you found me at St. Killian's, just like this," I say to Michael. "You took me downstairs, blindfolded me, and we heard things, just like this."

Chen groans, panting harder, and I can tell she's about to come.

"I loved your world," I whisper.

"You wanted to see so badly that day in the catacombs."

The heat of his body warms my skin. "I even think part of you wanted to be her. To experience it all."

"I wanted anything with you," I reply, opening my eyes. "I wanted to let it all happen."

Samara's body bobs back and forth, her back arching again and again as Lev buries his mouth in her pussy and she gets closer. Her moans fill the room, growing louder and faster.

"I wish I could go back to that night," I tell Michael. "I would've tried not to get in that truck. I would've tried not to steal all this time from you."

Tears burn behind my eyes. I'm a burden to him. I feel like I'm making his life worse.

But all of a sudden, his arms wrap around me, and his whisper hits my neck. "And if I could go back, I wouldn't have wasted a moment."

He lifts me off my feet, and I suck in a breath as he carries me back a few steps. He drops down, bringing me into his lap, and I realize he's in a chair. I still see slivers of the scene through the tanks, Lev rising and Samara panting and whimpering in protest that he stopped. He takes her legs, pulling her down to the end of the table as he unfastens his jeans.

Michael pulls me back against him, one arm around my body and one hand cupping my cheek as he whispers in my ear. "I would've left that warehouse that night, but I would've taken you with me instead."

An ache hits my heart, but also a flutter. I love how we love each other now, but if he had taken me with him that night—if I hadn't decided to walk home—so much might not have happened to keep us apart all that time.

"I would've kept my word," he goes on. "Just kissing you and holding you, and that would've been enough then,

71

because just the feel of you drove me out of my mind." His breath is hot on my skin, and I hear the desire in his voice. "I would've sat you down on the counter in my parents' dark kitchen that night, standing between your legs as I ate you up, because at any moment we could've been caught, and I wanted to get us into trouble. I wanted them to try to keep me from you the way they always did, only this time I wouldn't have listened."

Lev thrusts himself inside Samara, and I see David come from behind her, grabbing her arms and forcing them over her head as she gasps. She whimpers, but he covers her mouth with his before taking her breasts in his hands, squeezing them.

She pulls at his hold. "I'm scared."

"I know," David says. And then he sinks his mouth into her breast, not stopping.

But just as Lev starts going hard and Samara starts writhing under the attention of the two men, something comes down over my face, and I can barely breathe as Michael ties something around my eyes. The world goes black, and my heart pumps so hard, I want to smile and laugh and cry, because I'm too excited to know what to do. I raise my hand, feeling Michael's necktie wrapped around my eyes.

Lev grunts. "Ugh, fuck."

The table creaks on its bolts as moans and kissing fill the hot air of the engine room.

The camera starts clicking again as Alex takes her pictures. "Can David have his turn?" I hear Alex ask.

I don't hear an answer as she takes more pictures.

"I would've kissed you," Michael goes on, dragging his fingers along my jaw. "And touched your face and started sweating, because I was so hard, wanting something so sweet that I couldn't have yet."

The fabric of my dress chafes my breasts, and I nuzzle into him, breathing hard. *Touch me.* You can. I'm not sixteen anymore.

"I wouldn't have wanted to stop," he continues, "but I would've put you to bed, because the next time I came home from college you would've been seventeen." The tip of his tongue flicks my ear before he catches the lobe in his teeth and slips a hand inside my dress, cupping my breast.

I gasp.

"And I would've gone under the clothes then," he teases. "I would've snuck you into my room, taken off your panties, and touched you and let you touch me, and I would've kissed you everywhere, Rika." He kneads with one hand and spreads the slit of my skirt, baring my legs and naked pussy, teasing me with his fingers. "Everywhere."

"Michael..." I moan, picturing what could've been. The boys would never have gone to prison, and I would've been high, living for when Michael came home, because nothing feels as good as him wanting me.

"Please, stop stopping," Samara whines. "I need to come."

The table has stopped creaking, and I hear a shuffle of feet as Michael slides his fingers up and down my pussy, chaste and never dipping inside.

"My turn," I hear David say in the distance.

"It would've driven us crazy," Michael whispers, "and we would've come so close it hurt."

Doing everything we could right under our parents' noses but dying to do the one thing we couldn't.

"And when you turned eighteen," he tells me, the whispers seeping through my body and making my clit throb so hard, "I would've bided my time during the dinner and the fucking cake and the presents, and you wouldn't have been able to enjoy it, because you would've felt my eyes on you during the whole damn thing and known what was coming. They wouldn't have been able to find you. They would've been frantic, because I would've had you far away, down on the beach, in a tent, and I wouldn't have stopped...all night."

I bite my bottom lip, rubbing the tip of my nose against his cheek as I grind on him a little. The thick ridge of his cock pulses under me, and I take his hand between my legs and guide it down farther, pressing his fingers into the wetness on my inner thigh. A strap of the dress falls down, the air hitting my bare breast.

"Rika..." he growls under his breath.

"Michael."

The camera clicks another picture, but this time I see the flash through my blindfold. The skin of my nipples grows tight as they harden. Alex is here.

Michael rubs his thumb over my nipple, and my breath shakes. "And you wouldn't have turned up until I dropped you off for school the next morning," he goes on. "In front of everyone so they knew who the fuck had you now."

And he gives me a hard squeeze, making me gasp. Another picture and another flash.

I jerk, but instead of covering myself, I...

I like it. Chills spread across my skin, and I want more. I want to be looked at.

Alex snaps another picture, and I don't know what she sees or what she's focused on, but she's watching us now as Samara and David go at it on the other side of the tanks, and Michael touches me. Where's Lev? I still can't see, so I don't know.

"We wouldn't have made it through dinner, Michael," I whisper, breathing in his skin. "You would've felt me and known—all I wanted was you. I wouldn't have been able to wait anymore."

Michael takes my hand and guides two of my fingers down between my legs, sliding them inside of me. My pussy throbs, and I groan, needing so much more. He brings my hand back up and slips each finger into his mouth, sucking me off from them.

The camera snaps again as Michael's hot tongue glides slowly across my fingers. Samara cries out in the distance, coming.

But then, suddenly, a hot breath falls across my face, and I hear heavy breathing. My heart stops for a moment. Who is that?

"Do that again," Lev suddenly whispers, and I hear him swallow. "Please."

I pant, my heart hammering.

Oh, my God.

Michael holds my face, kissing my cheek, jaw, and neck. "Do you trust me?" he asks.

I...

I nod.

"Then why would you ever think the idea of children with any other woman wouldn't make me sick?" he whispers, and I can hear the pain in his voice. "We will have kids. If you want them. But I will never not have you." He shakes me. "Do you understand?"

A sob lodges in my throat.

"Do you understand?" he growls again. "A world where there is no us can't happen."

We kiss, and I barely notice as Michael takes my hand and dips it down between my legs again. *Oh, God.* I start to cry, but I calm myself, the heartache breaking me, and I don't know why. Why did I ever doubt him? I can live without a lot of things, but I can't live without him. Why did I not trust the same from him?

Pressing my two fingers inside me, he withdraws them and holds my hand up, not sucking on it, though.

"Do you trust me?" he asks again.

"Yes."

He holds my hand out, and I barely have a moment to register what's happening before Lev grabs my hand. I gasp as the flash clicks again. Slowly, the wet heat of his mouth covers my finger, and my mouth falls open as I whimper, his tongue making every hair on my body stand on end. Michael kneads my breast, possessive and breathing hard in my ear as Lev licks my fingers clean, gently biting them.

"I love watching you feel," Michael says. "I love your face."

Lev sucks the other finger clean, long and slow, and I know he's looking down at me. Michael squeezes me as he buries his whispers in my neck and grinds his cock under me.

"I can't follow the rules," he says, "and with you, I don't have to. I'm not alone. I can't go back to being alone." He hovers over my lips, our mouths open and hungry. "I can't fucking breathe without my little monster."

Little Monster.

I breathe out a half-laugh, half-cry. "I love you, Michael." I kiss him. "I love you so much."

He dives into my mouth, and I grab hold of the armrests to steady myself, but I grab Lev's wrists instead, his hands already wrapped around the arms of the chair. I don't move my hands off him.

"Do you trust me?" Michael breathes out.

"Forever."

"Stand up, Lev," Michael orders.

And before I know what's happening, he's pushing me forward to sit up in his lap, Lev catching me before I go too far. Michael yanks at the back of my dress, and I clutch the waist of Lev's jeans, the belt unfastened but still there. Michael rips the dress away from my body, more flashes going off from Alex's camera, and only the black, leather belt remains around my waist.

Lev's fingers caress my face, and I'm spinning behind the blindfold. "God, she's hot," he whispers. "Can I touch her?"

"No," Michael tells him, and I hear his belt fall open and then his zipper.

He grips my hips, jerks me back, and I moan, burying my face in Lev's stomach as Michael spreads my legs wider and sinks deep inside me.

I whimper, wrapping my arms around Lev for support. But I feel a bulge in his jeans and pull my head up.

He laughs under his breath. "Sorry."

Michael's cock stretches me, and I grip Lev's belt as I start rolling my hips and fucking Michael slow. He squeezes my body, pulling me back into his cock, while I roll forward, pulling myself into Lev. Our pace quickens.

Alex takes more shots, and I arch my back, feeling my hair drape down my skin.

Samara pants and cries from somewhere beyond the tanks, and I moan, the light layer of sweat on my back cooling me as Michael jerks me back harder and faster.

"Hold on to me," Lev says, and I feel him lower to his knees as he puts my hands on his shoulders. I can't see him, but he's close, his breath falling on my breast.

"Michael," he says, struggling. "Please let me taste her again."

Another flash goes off as Lev's mouth hovers over my nipple. I breathe hard, rocking back and forth into both men, my orgasm starting to crest already. I push off Lev into Michael and off of Michael, holding onto Lev.

"Ugh, fuck, Rika," Michael grunts, his fingers digging into my hips. He pumps his own up into me, and I can't hold back anymore.

"Yes," I moan. More pictures snap.

I bounce up and down on him, going deep and hard, my orgasm building and my moans and cries get louder. I rock back and forth, chasing it and then...it explodes, racing through my body, and I feel Michael grip the back of my hair, pulling my head back as he grunts and groans, Lev's hot mouth damn-near boiling over where it hovers over my nipple.

Oh, fuck. Fuck, fuck, fuck...

I writhe a little, groaning as the pleasure courses. A trickle of sweat glides down my back, and Michael loosens and tightens his fist in my hair as he spills inside of me, and I try to catch my breath, noticing the flashes have stopped.

God...

God, that was so good. I pull down my blindfold and lean back, diving into Michael's mouth again. Alex leans against one of the tanks, the camera dangling from her fingers as she watches us, photography forgotten.

Michael's still inside me, and I look between Alex and Lev, both of them looking at us like they can't tear their eyes away.

"Yo, Lev," I hear David call. "She wants more. Come on."

Lev smiles at me, his eyes peeking out from under his black hair, and he rises, leaning over me.

"At your service anytime, Miss Fane," he whispers.

His eyes flash to Michael, and then he turns and heads back to his own party.

Alex opens the slot on her camera and pulls out the memory card. She comes over, handing it to us.

"Look at them together some time," she tells us, and I take it.

She turns to head back, as well, but then she stops and looks over her shoulder at us. "And it's probably good that you didn't let Lev have that second taste."

I pinch my brows.

"He would've sucked you off Michael," she explains.

My eyes go wide, and I think Michael stops breathing. She grins and leaves, disappearing beyond the tanks.

It takes a moment to find my lungs, but all of a sudden, I break out in a quiet laugh.

Oh, my God. What would Michael have done? The image floats through my mind, and I don't hate it, actually. It might be incredible to see him experience something new for a change. Put the shoe on the other foot, so to speak?

But Michael clamps his hand over my mouth and whispers in my ear. "Don't even think about it," he warns.

I smile, rising from his lap, and he stands up, giving me his shirt, since my dress is ripped to shambles on the floor. I hear the camera click again as Samara goes for round three or four—I lost count—and Michael scoops up my dress and takes my hand, leading me out of the engine room.

I can't believe we just did that.

But then, I can. We don't have to hide around these people.

We climb the steps and make our way to the owner's deck, his warm hand gripping mine so tightly, like he's afraid I'll be lost.

"The wedding is in one month," he finally says, pulling me along.

I hold his white Oxford closed around my body. A month? I start to protest. "Michael, I can't..."

"One month." He turns to look at me. "Devil's Night. We have until then to find Will and get him back."

He grips my hand, leading us both down the corridor to our cabin, and we pass Winter and Damon's room, but all I can hear is muffled words and moans.

A month? I'm thrilled to have a date, but...

We'll be paying through the roof to have everything ready in time.

But still...

A month. I smile, hugging his arm like I do when I'm feeling sixteen and smitten with him all over again.

He swings open the door to the cabin, tossing his jacket and tie, and both of us head to the bathroom. I jump into the shower, him following me, and he holds me, kissing my forehead as the steam billows around us.

And I don't let go of him as he washes my hair and my body, barely blinking as I watch how good he loves me and how lucky we are.

After we get out, we dry off, and I let my hair down as he passes me my toothbrush with paste already on it. "I'm sorry I said those things earlier in the lounge," he tells me, the toothbrush in his mouth. "I was pissed. And intimidated. You weren't talking to me, and my pride was shot."

I start brushing as he spits, and I meet his eyes in the mirror. "I was lying to you. I'm sorry, too."

Omission is lying, and it was hurting us.

I finish up and rinse, patting my mouth dry with a hand towel. When I enter the room, he's dressed in a pair of lounge pants and sitting by the windows, smoke from a cigar billowing into the air above his head. It's so funny. Damon quits, and everyone else starts.

I slip on some white panties and a matching cami, walking over and sliding into his lap. I throw my legs over the arm of his chair as he cradles me, and I rest my head on his shoulder, watching the black sea spread out before us.

"No matter the money or the meetings or the mayor's office, Michael," I tell him, "I'll always be perpetually twelve. Searching for Trevor's older brother in every room I enter."

He never has to feel intimidated. Nothing is worth anything without him. I bury my head in his shoulder, his hold tightening around me.

"And I'm not wearing white to the wedding," I say sweetly.

Just so we're clear.

He snorts, and I smile, looking up to see him taking another drag.

"Yeah, me neither," he teases.

I run my hand up his beautiful chest, tracing the dips and muscles, and then circle my arms around his neck again and kiss him there. Nothing has really changed in all this time. His smell is like my matchboxes. It feels like Christmas and the Fourth of July together.

"I love you." I pause and then add, because I can't help myself, "Mr. Fane."

"Oh, Jesus, fuck," he grumbles and sits up. "I need a drink."

Huh? I hold tighter, damn-near falling off as he tries to get up from the chair.

"Off me, now," he orders. "I need a drink, Rika. Many drinks."

I slide to the floor, the carpet scraping against my ass. I wince. "Hey."

He pops the cigar in this mouth, shaking his head, and storms for the door.

Rika Crist just doesn't sound right. He's going to lose this one.

"We only have a weeks' supply of food on this boat!" I yell as he opens the door. "So, don't wait too long to come to terms with this!"

"Goodnight!" he barks. "I love you!"

And he leaves, the door slamming rather hard for someone who says he can't live without me.

I stare after him, a slow laugh rolling through me.

One month. I'm ready. I'm ready for it all.

And I smile, excitement coursing through me as I reach for my notebook on the table to make notes for the wedding planner.

THE END

Please continue reading if you'd
like to go back and revisit Iversen's birth!

Damon

THIS SCENE TAKES PLACE ABOUT TEN MONTHS AFTER THE END OF KILL SWITCH. ABOUT A YEAR BEFORE CONCLAVE.

"You're insane!" Bryce screamed, walking away but then turning back around and charging up to me again. "I'm going, and I'm not coming back this time!"

'K, bye.

I slid the notch of the hammer onto the nail head, pulling out the nail and removing his full morning of fuck-ups. The muscles in my arms were charged and hot, and if he didn't fucking leave, I'd remove him myself.

"I mean it, Damon!" he barked again, calling my bluff.

I shot him a middle finger, not looking at him.

I heard cans crash to the floor and guessed he'd probably kicked something as he stormed to the door.

"Hey, what the hell?" I heard Kai burst in, the two-way door flapping as he charged in from the front office and into the warehouse where we were working. "What's going on?"

"He's crazy," Bryce said. "He can't work with people!"

I laughed under my breath.

I heard Kai sigh, because he was as much at his wits' end as I was.

Like, seriously. No one here could think for themselves. You had to tell them every little goddamn thing, and

God help you if you had to give them more than one instruc-
tion at a time, because their brains would fucking short out
because they couldn't remember all that AND remember to
breathe at the same time.

I finished removing the last two nails and pulled the
two by four off and tossed it to the side, getting rid of any
evidence he did any work here today.

"He's temperamental, but he'll compromise," Kai explained to Bryce. "We've been through this before."

"Compromise?" Bryce whined. "He threw an ax at my
head!"

"If I'd thrown it at your head, I would've hit your
head," I growled low.

There was silence, and then I heard Bryce's voice. "I'm
outta here, man."

I knelt down, pulling up the nails on the next board
he'd fucked up.

"Bryce, come on."

"Let him go," I told Kai.

The door swung open again, hitting the wall, and the
rest of the crew around me cleared their throats, getting
back to work as Kai loomed. Why was he even fucking here?
If I couldn't have Will handling shit out there, then I wanted one of the girls. Michael and Kai stressed me out more.

"How are you going to get anything done?" Kai de-
manded, and I noticed a stack of papers crunched in his fist.

"A lot better without that idiot around."

"Damon..."

But I shook my head. *Just fucking stop.* I needed to get
the framing done on three more treehouses before the baby
came in like nine days, not to mention finalize the design
on the fountain in front of Meridian City's new library *and*
figure out what the fuck a she-shed was, because Catherine

O'Reilly just loved her son's new treehouse and thought I could build her something of her own. She was paying double to rush it before the snow started in a few months, so I couldn't say no.

Photographers were coming by all week to get shots of "work-in-progress" for the new website that Alex was handling, and thankfully doing everything to get us set up online. I just wanted people to leave me alone in the warehouse. I moved faster without help here.

But part me knew I was part of my own problem, too. The Langston kid wanted a treehouse, but once I found out he was obsessed with pirates I chucked everything that was already done and started a design for a tallship instead. What the fuck was I thinking?

I looked over at the bow and masts already constructed, feeling a smile tug at my lips. It was going to look fucking fantastic when it was done, though. It was worth it if he loved it.

"You are running on fumes," Kai told me. "You just got back from Washington, and then California before that, you have a baby on the way, projects are piling up..." He trailed off, and I felt him inch closer. "I can't believe I'm saying this, but I think you should start smoking again."

I arched an eyebrow. I hadn't entirely quit, actually. I probably never would.

Lifting up the first frame, I leaned it against the wall and then moved to the next one.

"You don't need employees, you need a team," Kai said, following me. "I'm not taking any more orders until we get this place in shape. With a regular staff. I've already put word out at the university that you're recruiting."

I shot him a scowl. He wasn't wrong. I just didn't have time to deal with it.

But Kai went on, "You need an office manager, you need a design team, and you need a receptionist, and that's not me. I have enough on my plate." He rubbed his neck. "Everyone is scrambling to keep you covered, but you'll be a lot less stressed if your home base is running smoothly."

"Fine, whatever," I snapped. "Just take care of it. I need to stay ahead of schedule."

Just do what you want, and don't bug me with it. I knew they were all doing me a shitload of favors, and I was grateful they were here, because I wasn't cut out for a lot of this. I just wanted someone else to be the face of the business and for me to stay in the background, designing and building and being left alone. If Will was here, he could do it. He'd be happy to do it.

But he wasn't here a lot lately. He'd come home for a couple months and then fly off again, itching for space he never seemed to need before. He, Alex, and a few others were backpacking around Scandinavia over the summer, but when they came home, he stayed there, and I hadn't seen him in weeks.

Although, he checked in regularly.

I think he was feeling left out. He saw Michael with Rika, Kai with Banks, and me with Winter, and struggled to feel like he belonged. He had Alex, but she wasn't what he needed, and he just kept running away again and again, so he wouldn't think or...feel. Or deal.

Kai turned and headed back for the lobby, but then stopped, pulling his phone out of his pocket.

"Ah, shit," he said. "Where's your phone?"

"Why?" I grumbled.

"Because it's time."

"Time for what?"

He stared at his phone, smiling to himself. "I guess your girlfriend likes to stay ahead of schedule, too." And he looked up at me. "She went into labor two hours ago. Where's your fucking phone?"

My heart leapt into my throat. What?! I patted my jeans, looking around me.

Shit!

I spotted it laying on a pile of boards and darted over, swiping it up. Pressing the power button, it didn't light up.

"Fuck, it's dead. Where is she?" I barked.

Two hours. She'd been in labor for two hours?!

But he just laughed. "At the hospital. Let's go."

Why was he laughing? Maybe he forgot how frantic he was when his kid came a few months ago.

I charged out of the room, hearing Kai tell the guys to lock the place up at five, and we hurried out of the building and into my car.

• • •

We rushed into the hospital, knowing Labor and Delivery was on the third floor from when Banks had her kid in May. I didn't even know Winter was in the city today. What the hell's the matter with me? She probably texted, but I'd forgotten to charge my phone last night, and I didn't know how long it had been dead.

We went up the elevator and bolted out as soon as the doors opened, heading for the nurses' station, but I immediately spotted Banks sitting on some chairs, holding her and Kai's son.

Madden.

Mads, for short. Mads Mori. Poor kid sounded like an assassin.

I brushed her face as I walked by, and she smiled big, excited for me. Mads gnawed with his toothless mouth on her jaw, making cute sounds and shit.

But then a scream pierced the air and a gasp, and I heard a man's voice and Alex's coaching. "I've got you!"

Without waiting, I burst into the room, my heart jumping into my throat. I'd never heard Winter sound like that before. *Jesus.* Was it supposed to sound like that?

She laid on the bed, and I rushed up to her, helping Alex hold her up as she pushed for the doctor.

"Six, seven, eight…" the nurse continued counting.

"Baby," I breathed out, kissing her.

"Damon," she gasped, realizing I was here.

"Nine, ten," they finished.

And Winter let out a breath, sucking in air.

"I was so scared you weren't going to be here," she said. "My water broke while we were shopping, and he's coming so fast."

"I was with her," Alex told me.

I steeled my arms around Winter and kissed her forehead, cheeks, and lips, making sure she felt me close.

"Thanks," I told Alex.

Winter shook, and I studied her face, seeing her biting her bottom lip and tears hanging at the corner of her eyes.

And just like that, she was eight again, our fingers hanging on by a thread in the treehouse, and I couldn't stop what was happening to her.

"Why is she crying?" I barked at the doctor.

"Because it fucking hurts!" she yelped, answering for him.

"Well, give her something!"

"It's too late for that now," he mumbled through his mask and then peered over Winter's legs. "Plus, you wanted natural childbirth, right?"

"What the fuck for?" I burst out, looking down at her like she had three heads. "We didn't talk about that."

She growled and pushed back up on her elbows.

"All right, deep breath and push!" the doctor said. "One, two, three, four..."

"Ahhh!" she gritted through her teeth, her whole fucking body tense and rigid, and I wanted to look, but I didn't want to leave her.

"Five, six, seven..." they called.

Winter looked flushed and sweat beaded her brow.

"Eight, nine..."

Her face twisted up, and she let out a small scream, and a tear fell, and I tightened my fists, unable to take my eyes off her. *Jesus, fuck.* Why the hell would she turn down perfectly legal drugs?

"Ok, the head is out!" the doctor told us.

My lungs emptied, and my stomach somersaulted. I moved to look, but she pulled me back. "Don't leave me."

I leaned back down and kissed her, but I started to laugh, and I couldn't help it.

I didn't know why I was feeling what I was feeling, but it was incredible. Whatever it was.

"I'll bet it's a boy," she said, sucking in deep breaths.

"If you're wrong, you have to do that bathtub thing for me," I remind her of our bet.

We hadn't found out the sex of the kid, wanting to be surprised.

But she just laughed despite herself. "I do it for you anyway. You know that?" she shot back.

"Ok, one more push," the doctor told her.

Alex and I lifted her up again, and she took a few deep breaths, and then inhaled one more and held it, squeezing her eyes shut and pushing as the count began.

"One, two, three..."

I stared at her face, so much shit washing over me as I watched her, but most of all I just wanted to hold her close. I couldn't believe this was happening.

"Four, five..."

I was going to be such a screw up. I'd do so many things wrong with her and this kid.

"Six, seven, eight..."

But fuck, I was going to love them. I didn't care about being perfect. I just wanted to be everything my father wasn't. I wanted this with her a million more times, and no matter all the shit that still lived inside me, I already knew I was better than him.

"Nine, ten..."

The doctor pulled back, Winter collapsed, and I heard a shrill cry fill the room.

"It's a boy!" the doctor said.

I looked over, seeing red, little arms and legs as they cleared out his mouth and checked him, and then I watched as they brought him over and put him on Winter's chest with a little blanket.

She smiled but started crying, wrapping her arms around him, and I just stood there, unable to breathe for a minute.

"A boy," she said. "Told you."

"Jesus Christ." I smiled, lightly touching his head, almost afraid to touch him. "Holy shit."

I checked his fingers and counted his toes, holding one of his long legs as he kicked.

"Twenty-two and three-fourths inches long, eight pounds and eleven ounces," the nurse said somewhere behind us.

"That's big," the doctor commented. "He's going to play basketball, Damon."

I smiled but didn't take my eyes off my girl and my kid.

I kind of wished we were fucking married now, but with the business, Winter's dancing, and the pregnancy, we decided to take our time and do it right. I wanted to have it our way.

Alex left, probably to tell everyone waiting that he was here and healthy, and then I remembered that Will wasn't here.

I faltered. He should be here for this. Out of all my friends, he should be here.

"What does he look like?" Winter whispered up at me, her voice raspy.

I smoothed my hand over both their heads. "Like next year he'll be running around in the fountains with us," I told her. "He's perfect, baby. Black hair, a little pissed off..."

She snorted, and I thought about what he'd look like in a year when he was walking and running and laughing and playing. I wanted the noise. I wanted it all over the house. I wanted it filling our lives from here on out.

"Congratulations," the doctor said as the nurses cleared up.

I kept my eyes on my kid. "How soon can she get pregnant again?" I asked the doctor.

"Damon..." Winter laughed under her breath.

I heard the doctor chuckle. "I think he likes being a father," he said to Winter.

But I just turned my head and locked eyes with the doctor, and his face fell.

"Oh, you're serious," he said, realizing I wasn't laughing.

He opened his mouth to speak, but it took him a few moments to find his words. "Um, within a few months, I'd say," he finally answered. "It was a healthy pregnancy. But she needs time to heal."

And then he said it again, slower and firmer, sounding like a warning. "You should give her time to heal."

The corner of my mouth tipped up, amused.

Did he think I was a monster?

• • •

The night passed as they transferred Winter into another room and took the baby to get washed. When they returned him, we all held him for a while, and Banks, Kai, Michael, and Rika finally left, but I asked Alex to stay in case Winter needed something, and we didn't want to leave her alone. I stayed by his bassinet, watching him breathe as mother and son both slept, but after not being able to get any myself, I needed to stretch my legs.

I walked over to Winter, pulling my phone off the charger as I whispered in her ear. "Going to get some air," I told her. "Be right back."

She moaned softly and nodded, and I left, closing the door behind me.

I went down the elevator and made my way outside, the balmy August air thick and heavy on my skin as I stretched my arms over my head and yawned. I breathed in the smell of hot asphalt and fresh bread from the bakery down the street and dialed Will, but it went straight to voicemail.

I shook my head.

I almost hung up, but then a rush of sudden anger made me lash out. "You knew my kid was coming this month," I snapped. "Why aren't you here? You missed it. You know, you're just really fucking..."

But I stopped and hung up, grinding my teeth together, because I didn't know what to say.

Asshole.

But after a moment, I felt bad. I had no right to lose my temper with him.

I dialed him back, waiting for voicemail to pick up again. "I miss you," I said. "We all miss you. We need you, okay? My son needs you. You're his favorite. I know it already. Just..."

I shook my head again and hung up.

I shouldn't be angry. I'd done my fair share of shit I thought I needed to do.

This was just important. I wanted him part of this memory.

I turned to go back inside, but a twinge of something else hit my nostrils, and I paused. Realization hit, and I smiled to myself, forgetting Will for a moment.

Turning my head, I saw a cloud of smoke drift from behind a corner and walked toward it, spotting Rika sitting on a parking stump with her legs outstretched and ankles crossed as she smoked a Davidoff.

I walked up next to her, staying standing, and without looking, she handed me the pack and lighter as if expecting me.

What was she up to? She'd been awkward as fuck the past several months, and I was half-tempted to kidnap her again, steal Michael's yacht, and take her to sea until she had it out with me. We hadn't gotten a chance to speak earlier, but she was clearly back for a reason.

I took the cigarettes and dug one out, lighting the tip and reveling in the welcome, familiar taste. I took another puff and blew out the smoke, handing the cigarettes and lighter back to her.

"I'm going to tell her she has a grandchild," she stated, still staring ahead.

So that was why she was sitting out here at four in the morning? Trying to figure out how to handle a situation that was none of her damn business?

"Tell her whatever you want."

In the months since I'd found out that Rika's mother was also mine, I'd neither spoken to nor reached out to Christiane Fane. She saw to my freedom after my father was killed, but as far as I was concerned, she owned me that much, so no, I wasn't grateful. Screw her.

Winning wasn't important, but the fight was, and she didn't fight for me at all. Having her around would bring absolutely nothing to the table.

But Rika continued to protest. "Damon, you can't do this to her. She deserves to be in his life."

"Do you really believe that?" I asked her even though she still wouldn't look at me. "What if my father had never told me the truth? Would she have? It didn't look like that was her plan."

"Maybe once she learned he was dead, that was exactly her plan," she shot back. And then she stood up and looked up at me. "The truth is, she wanted you. She didn't abort you or give you away. And she wasn't the best mother she could be, but she never hurt me. She never raised a hand to me, and she loved me."

I shook my head, not caring.

Or trying not to care.

An image of Christiane played in my head, though. Young, crying, holding me in her arms before my father snatches me away. I couldn't imagine the pain.

But I blinked and shook my head. No. I was a parent now, and I knew, without a doubt, nothing would stand between him and me. She was weak for far too long. My kid didn't need someone like that.

"She's not the only family you have, either," Rika pointed out. "She comes with an army of relatives in Africa and Europe. Don't you want that for your children?"

"No," I retorted without hesitation. "My children will have Winter and me." And then I looked over at her. "And you."

She narrowed her eyes on me.

"And Banks, Alex, and the guys," I added. "And they'll have your children. This is their family. It's exactly the family I want for them."

And before she could argue any more, I flicked the cigarette off and walked away, back toward the entrance.

"I will win this," she called out, threatening me.

And I turned around, unable to hide the smile from my face. "I look forward to seeing your next move," I taunted.

And I spun back around, heading into the hospital.

Honestly, I wasn't concerned. She might win, but it wouldn't be tonight, and it wouldn't happen if I didn't ultimately want it to. The prospect of having Rika back in play was just too much fun, though, so let her try.

I hated my father for everything he'd done, but even though I hated to admit it, I loved this part. Part of me always wondered why I was drawn to Rika just a little more than other women besides Winter and Banks. I wondered why whatever was between us felt natural and inevitable. How I could've hurt her or killed her a thousand times, but something always held me back.

Of course, she was one of my own. Of course, she was. It all made sense last Devil's Night. Everything seemed to align, and I had no fear.

Like Banks—like Winter and me—Rika was unique. She was built for the wilds, and I wanted her in my family.

Walking back down the hall and heading up in the elevator, I made my way for Winter's room and lightly closed the door behind me. Her phone sat on the bedside table, an app playing some rain sounds as she slept, and I stepped over, looking in the bassinet at the sleeping baby, who was still swaddled up tight and warm. But now he wore a black beanie with white lettering "New to the Crew."

I laughed quietly and looked over at Alex passed out on the chair next to his little bed. I didn't remember that among any of the things Winter bought. I'd have to thank Alex. That was pretty funny. She must've woken up and changed it while I was outside.

I cocked my head, looking down at him. I expected him to be crying 24/7, but he was pretty quiet. Maybe he knew he was safe.

Or maybe he was tired, and shit would get real tomorrow.

"How is he?" I heard Winter whisper.

I popped up, looking over and seeing her sit up, her blonde hair in beautiful disarray around her.

"Asleep," I told her.

I leaned down and held her face, noticing how exhausted she looked. We were both running on little fuel with everything going on these days, and it was time to slow down. I'd wanted to get so much more done before the kid came, but there was no time for that now. She'd need me a lot the next couple of weeks, at least. But eventually, I'd need to hire someone to help with the baby. We knew that was a reality.

For now, though, I'd enjoy it just being the three of us.

I kissed her, and she put her hand on mine. "I need a shower."

I stood up and took her hands. "I'll help."

I guided her out of the bed and carefully across the suite to the bathroom, leaning down to nudge Alex on the way. "Alex?" I said, seeing her jostle. "Keep an ear out for the kid, okay? We're gonna take a shower."

She nodded and yawned, and we headed into the bathroom, but I left the door open a crack, just in case.

Winter wasted no time shedding her hospital gown as I started the shower, getting the water warm enough, and she wrapped her arms around my waist, hanging onto me like she was going to fall over.

"You smell like high school," she mused.

"I had a cigarette," I admitted, even though I was pretty sure she knew I was still smoking here and there. "I was just feeling too good."

"I like it."

I didn't want it all over my clothes when I held the kid, but the prospect of looking forward to a smoke once in a while made "quitting" easier.

I stripped off my clothes and lifted her into the shower with me, closing the door behind us.

As soon as I put her under the water, I saw the blood start to rinse from her body and turn the floor pink.

My stomach turned a little. I wanted more kids, but I didn't like putting her body through this at all. I knew she'd be fine once she healed, but it almost seemed unfair that some women did this five or six times. Sometimes more. It looked brutal.

And I didn't want to see her cry like that again.

We washed our hair and rinsed, and then I soaped up a cloth and washed her body, knowing she must be fucking sore to let me do it without protest.

"What will you do?" she asked as I knelt in front of her and washed her legs. "About Christiane?"

I paused, thinking. With Rika, I had too much pride to give myself away, but with Winter, I was freer.

"Do you think I should let her in?" I asked, not looking at her.

She put her hands on my shoulders to steady herself as I lifted her leg and washed her foot.

"I don't think we have to be in a hurry to make any decisions now," she said.

I smiled to myself. I loved how she was. She made me better, because I loved seeing her happy, but she didn't push me, either.

"Our family comes first," she added.

"Our family..." I repeated. *My family. Mine.*

I continued washing her, finishing her legs and cleaning the blood off her thighs.

"Do you ever stand at the edge of a cliff or a balcony," she asked, "and have this moment where you wonder what it would feel like to jump?"

I raised my eyebrows.

"Kind of thrilled at the idea that you're one step from death?" She squeezed my shoulders. "One step..." she said. "And everything changes?"

"Yeah," I said quietly. "It symbolizes a need to engage in self-destructive behavior. It's not that uncommon."

While driving, we think, even for just a moment, about jerking the steering wheel into oncoming traffic or leaping off the balcony of a ship and into the abyss of the black water below. They're passing thoughts and little dares we allow our psyche, because we're tired of not living and we want the fear. We want to remember why we want to live.

And some of us were more tempted than others at the thrill of how, in the moment, everything could change. Of how it's not about who we are but what we are, and animals don't apologize for whatever they need to do to survive.

"There's a French phrase for it," she said. "L'appel du vide."

I looked up at her, her pink lips misty with hot water.

"That's what binds us," she told me.

"Who?"

"Our family."

Our family?

"Kai, Banks, Michael, Rika, Will, Alex..." she went on. "You and me. We all hear it. L'appel du vide. The call of the void."

I stopped, gazing at her.

"The call of the void," I murmured.

Was she right? Was that what bound us together? Like recognizes like, after all, and we lived in that need to go a step further and feel everything we were capable of. The fear was terrifying, but coming out the other side redefined our reality.

"I like it," I told her.

She paused and then said, "I love you."

A pang hit my heart like it always did when she said that. Like I was falling for her all over again.

I stood up and wrapped my arms around her, smoothing her hair back under the water.

"You're so beautiful," I said. "Even though you gave me a son when I explicitly asked for a daughter."

She broke out in a laugh. "I didn't give you anything!" she argued. "It's the chromosome the male contributes that decides the child's sex. This is all your fault."

We both smiled, and I nudged her with my nose. I wasn't sure why I thought the kid was going to be a girl.

Maybe I just hoped. I seemed to be better with girls. Banks, Winter, Rika… I was afraid, I guess.

"We'll just have to keep trying," I teased.

She nuzzled into my neck, leaving little kisses and making chills break out all over my body.

"I love you," she whispered. "I love you."

My dick started to harden, and I shook my head. "Don't…" I begged. "You're going to make these next few weeks torture."

We couldn't have sex for I didn't know how long.

"He's perfect, you know?" I scaled my hands down her back. "You did an amazing job. I just hope he has more you than me in him."

She nodded, agreeing, and I gave her a swat on the ass.

She laughed. "So what are we naming him, then?" she asked.

"We didn't decide?"

"Not that I remember."

I closed my eyes, shaking my head. God, I had no idea. Nothing old, please. And nothing biblical.

Oh, and nothing unisex. Like Peyton, Leighton, or Drayton.

"Any ideas?" she asked.

But I just leaned her back into the wall and held her close. "Tomorrow," I said.

Right now I was more interested in climbing into bed with her and sleeping for as long as we could.

The name wasn't important. He had my hair, and tomorrow, maybe I'd get to see if he had her eyes.

If he had mine, then I guess nothing skipped generations, after all, and Christiane was full of it.

Couldn't wait to find out.

Thank you for reading!

ABOUT THE AUTHOR

Penelope Douglas is a New York Times, USA Today, and Wall Street Journal bestselling author. She grew up in Dubuque, Iowa and attended the University of Northern Iowa, studying political science. She then earned a graduate degree in Education from Loyola University New Orleans. She has four younger siblings, lives with her husband and daughter in New England, and loves breakfast, gin, and Hannibal Lecter. She does not drink gin for breakfast, but she *might* eat breakfast at Hannibal's.

Her books have been translated into more than twenty languages and include The Fall Away Series, The Devil's Night Series, and the standalones, Punk 57, Birthday Girl, and Credence, among others. Please look for the new standalone, Five Brothers, coming July 2024, and the next installment in the Hellbent series, QUIET ONES, coming soon!

Text DOUGLAS to 603-519-3800
to be alerted when a new book is live! (US Only)
Follow on social media!
Instagram: https://www.instagram.com/
penelope.douglas/
Spotify: https://open.spotify.com/user/pendouglas
TikTok: https://vm.tiktok.com/TTPdSskp6R/
BookBub: https://www.bookbub.com/profile/
penelope-douglas
Facebook: https://www.facebook.com/
PenelopeDouglasAuthor

Goodreads: http://bit.ly/1xvDwau
Website: https://pendouglas.com/
Email: penelopedouglasauthor@hotmail.com

And all of Pen's stories have Pinterest boards!
https://www.pinterest.com/penelopedouglas/

Made in United States
Orlando, FL
18 November 2024

53784563R00071